PUSHKIN PRE:
In association wit
WALTER PRESEN

THE
MYSTERY OF
HENRI PICK

In a world where we have so much choice, curation is becoming increasingly key. Walter Presents was first set up to champion brilliant drama from around the world and bring it to a wider audience.

Now, in collaboration with Pushkin Press, we're hoping to do the same thing for foreign literature: translating brilliant books into English, introducing them to readers who are hungry for quality fiction.

I discovered Henri Pick in a Parisian bookshop whilst waiting for a train. The characters and setting are quintessentially French and the mystery that lies at the heart of the book has instant international appeal. It's a charming plot, full of twists and turns, which will keep you guessing to the very last page. A perfect first selection for the Walter Presents Library.

Walter

Novelist, screenwriter and director **David Foenkinos** was born in 1974. He is the author of fourteen novels that have been translated into forty languages. Several of his works have been adapted for film, including *Delicacy* (2011).

Sam Taylor is a literary translator and novelist. He has written four novels, which have been translated into 10 languages, and translated more than 50 books from French including Laurent Binet's *The Seventh Function of Language* and Hubert Mingarelli's *Four Soldiers*, both longlisted for the International Booker Prize, and Leila Slimani's bestselling *Lullaby*.

THE
MYSTERY OF
HENRI PICK

DAVID
FOENKINOS

TRANSLATED FROM THE FRENCH
BY SAM TAYLOR

PUSHKIN PRESS
In association with
WALTER PRESENTS

Pushkin Press
71–75 Shelton Street
London WC2H 9JQ

The Mystery of Henri Pick was first published as *Le Mystère
Henri Pick* by Editions Gallimard in Paris, 2016

First published by Pushkin Press in 2020

5 7 9 8 6

ISBN 13: 978-1-78227-582-4

Epigraph: Ernst Cassirer qtd in Fritz Saxl, "Ernst Cassirer", in
The Philosophy of Ernst Cassirer, ed. Paul A. Schilpp (Tudor, 1958), p. 47

Quotation on p. 11 from Richard Brautigan, *The Abortion: An
Historical Romance 1966* (Vintage, 2002), p. 13 and p. 38

Quotations on p. 119 and p. 241 from Alexander Pushkin, *Yevgeny Onegin*,
translated by Anthony Briggs (Pushkin Press, 2016) p. 73

Designed and typeset by Tetragon, London
Printed and bound by CPI Group (UK) Ltd, Croydon, CR0 4YY

www.pushkinpress.com

THE
MYSTERY OF
HENRI PICK

"This library is dangerous."

ERNST CASSIRER,
on the Warburg Library

PART ONE

I

I N 1971, the American writer Richard Brautigan published *The Abortion: An Historical Romance 1966*, a quirky love story about a male librarian and a young woman with a spectacular body. In a way, the woman is the victim of her body, as if beauty were a curse. Vida—for that is the heroine's name—explains that a man was killed in a car accident because of her; mesmerized by the sight of this incredible passer-by, he simply forgot that he was driving. After the crash, the woman ran over to the car. The driver, covered in blood, managed to utter two last words before he died: "You're beautiful."

In fact, though, Vida's story is less important than the librarian's. Because the novel's most distinctive feature is that the library where he works will accept any book rejected by a publisher. For example, we meet one man who deposits his manuscript there after receiving four hundred rejection slips. All kinds of different books accumulate in this way, from an essay such as "Growing Flowers by Candlelight in Hotel Rooms" to a cookery book compiling every meal eaten in Dostoevsky's novels. One advantage of this arrangement is that the author can choose the spot on the shelf where his book will sit. He can leaf through the pages of his unfortunate colleagues before finding his place in this sort of anti-posterity. On the other hand, no manuscripts sent by post are accepted. The author must come in person to deliver the unwanted tome, as if to symbolize the final act of its absolute abandonment.

A few years later, in 1984, the author of *The Abortion* committed suicide in Bolinas, California. We will return to Brautigan's life and the circumstances that drove him to suicide a little later, but for now let us concentrate on that library, born in his imagination. In the early 1990s his idea became a reality: one of his fans created a "library of rejected books" in tribute to the deceased author, and the Brautigan Library began to accept the world's literary orphans. First located in the United States, it is now housed in Vancouver, Canada.[1] Brautigan would surely have been moved by this initiative, although obviously it is hard to know how a dead person would feel about anything. When the library was first founded, it made the news in several countries, including France. A librarian in Crozon, Brittany, decided to do the same thing, and in October 1992 he created a French version of the library of rejects.

2

Jean-Pierre Gourvec was proud of the small sign hanging outside his library: a quote by Emil Cioran, an ironic choice for a man who had practically never left his native Brittany:

1 For more information, go to www.thebrautiganlibrary.org

12

"Paris is the ideal place to mess up your life."

Gourvec was one of those men who prefer their region to their country, without descending into nationalistic fervour. His appearance might suggest otherwise: a tall, lean man with bulging neck veins and a very red complexion, Gourvec looked like someone with a very short fuse. But in fact he was a calm, thoughtful person, for whom words had a meaning and a destination. It took only a few minutes in his company for your false first impression to be replaced by another feeling: here was a man capable of withdrawing into himself like a Russian doll.

It was he who altered the layout of his bookshelves to create a space, at the back of the municipal library, for the world's homeless manuscripts. That rearrangement brought back to his mind a line by Jorge Luis Borges: "If you pick up a book in a library and put it back again, you tire out the shelves." They must be exhausted today, thought Gourvec with a smile. He had the sense of humour of an erudite man: a solitary, erudite man. That was how he saw himself, and it wasn't far from the truth. Gourvec was endowed with a minimal dose of sociability; he rarely laughed at the same things that made his neighbours laugh, although he would pretend to whenever they told a joke. Sometimes he would even go for a beer in the bar at the end of the street, where he'd talk about everything and nothing with the other men—particularly about nothing, he thought—and in those moments of collective excitement he would occasionally agree to play cards. It didn't bother him to be seen as a man like other men.

Little was known about his life, other than the fact that he lived alone. He had been married in the 1950s, but his wife had left him after only a few weeks and nobody knew why. It was said that he'd encountered her through a lonely hearts ad; they had written to each other for a long time before finally meeting. Was that the reason that their marriage failed? Gourvec was perhaps the kind of man whose written declarations of love were wonderful to read, so good that you were willing to give up everything for them, but behind the beauty of his words the reality was inevitably disappointing. Some malicious gossips at the time had claimed that his impotence was to blame for his wife's untimely departure. This theory seems improbable, but when the psychology of a situation is complex, people like to stick to the basics. In truth, nobody ever solved the mystery of that failed romance.

He had no long-term relationships after his wife left, and he never fathered children. It is difficult to know what his sex life was like. One might imagine him as the lover of neglected wives—the Emma Bovarys of his time. Some must have sought a deeper satisfaction between his bookshelves than mere words on a page. With this man who was a good listener—because he was a good reader—it was possible for a woman to escape the banal confines of her life. But there is no proof of any of this. One thing is certain: Gourvec's enthusiasm and passion for his library never faded. He gave his full attention to every customer, striving to listen carefully to what they said so that he could create a personal journey through his book recommendations. According to him, it was not a question of liking or not liking to read, but of finding the book that was meant for you. Everybody could love reading, as long as they had the right book in their hands, a book that spoke to them, a book they could not bear to part with. For this purpose, he had developed a method that might appear almost paranormal: he would examine each reader's physical appearance in order to work out which author they needed.

The ceaseless energy he put into making his library dynamic forced him to keep making it bigger. In his eyes, this was an immense victory, as if the books of the world formed an ever-diminishing army, and every act of resistance against their planned extinction was a kind of revolution. The Crozon mayor's office even agreed that he could hire an assistant. He placed an ad in the jobs section of the local newspaper. Gourvec enjoyed choosing which books to order, organizing the shelves and many other activities, but the idea of making a decision about *a human being* terrified him. All the same, he nurtured hopes of finding someone who would be a literary accomplice, someone with whom he could chat for hours about the use of ellipsis in the works of Céline, or quibble over the reasons for Thomas Bernhard's suicide. There was only one obstacle to this ambition: he knew perfectly well that he would be incapable of saying no to anybody. So the process would be simple: the person he hired would be the first one to apply. That was how Magali Croze came to join the library, thanks to the inarguable quality of having been quicker than anyone else to respond to the job offer.

3

Magali was not particularly fond of reading[2] but, as the mother of two young boys, she needed to find work as soon as possible. Particularly since her husband had only a part-time job at the Renault garage. In the early 1990s, fewer and fewer cars were being built in France, and the economic situation showed no signs of improving. As she signed her contract, Magali thought about her husband's hands, which were always smeared with grease. At least, handling books all day, that was one unpleasantness she was likely to avoid. It would be a fundamental difference in their marriage; her hands and her husband's were now on diametrically opposed trajectories.

When all was said and done, Gourvec liked the idea of working with someone for whom books were not sacred. It was possible, he acknowledged, to have a very good relationship with a colleague without discussing German literature every morning. He took care of recommending books to customers and she dealt with the logistics; as a working partnership, they were nicely balanced. Magali was not the kind of employee who questioned her boss's initiatives, but she couldn't help expressing her doubts when it came to all these rejected books.

"What's the point of stocking books that nobody wants?"

2   When he first laid eyes on her, Gourvec immediately thought: she looks like someone who would adore *The Lover* by Marguerite Duras.

16

"It's an American idea."

"So?"

"It's a tribute to Brautigan."

"Who?"

"Richard Brautigan. Haven't you read *Dreaming of Babylon*?"

"No. But anyway, it's a weird idea. And do you really want them to bring their books here? We'll get stuck with all the psychopaths in the area. Writers are mad, everybody knows that. And ones who aren't published... they must be even worse."

"They'll finally have a place. Think of it as charity work."

"I get it: you want me to be the Mother Teresa of failed writers."

"Yeah. Something like that."

"..."

Magali gradually came around to the idea, and tried to bring a positive attitude to the new venture. Jean-Pierre Gourvec ran an ad in some trade magazines, notably *Lire* and *Le Magazine Littéraire*, inviting all authors who wished to deposit their manuscript in the library of rejects to visit Crozon. The idea quickly took off, and many people made the journey. Writers came from all over France to rid themselves of the fruits of their failure. It was a sort of literary pilgrimage. There was a symbolic value in travelling hundreds of miles to put an end to the frustrations of not being published. Their words were erased, like sins. And perhaps there was something symbolic, too, about the name of the *département* where Crozon was located: Finistère, the ends of the earth.

4

In the ten years that followed, the library welcomed nearly a thousand manuscripts. Jean-Pierre Gourvec spent his time observing them, fascinated by the power of this useless treasure. In 2003, he became seriously ill and was hospitalized for a long time in Brest. This was doubly harsh in his eyes: his failing physical health bothered him less than being torn away from his books. He continued sending Magali instructions from his hospital bed, keeping his finger on the pulse of the literary world so he would know which books to order. He didn't want to miss anything. He poured the last of his strength into his lifelong passion. The library of rejected books no longer seemed to interest anybody, and that made him sad. After the excitement of its beginning, it was kept alive now only by word of mouth. In the United States too, the Brautigan Library was starting to flounder. Authors were no longer abandoning their unwanted books there.

When Gourvec returned from the hospital, he was much thinner. You didn't need to be a fortune teller to realize that he did not have long left to live. The town's inhabitants, in a sort of kindly reflex, were seized by a sudden desire to borrow books. Magali had fomented this artificial bookmania, understanding that it was the one thing that would make Jean-Pierre happy. Weakened by his illness, he didn't suspect that there was anything unnatural about this sudden surge of readers. On the contrary, he let himself believe that his long years of hard work were finally bearing fruit. He would leave the world soothed by this satisfying knowledge.

Magali also asked several of her acquaintances to quickly write a novel so that they could fill the shelves of the library of rejected books. She even got her mother involved.

"But I've never written anything in my life."

"Exactly. It's time you did. Write down your memories."

"But I don't remember anything. And I've committed so many sins."

"Nobody cares, Mama. We need books. Even your grocery list will do."

"Oh really? You think people would be interested in that?"

"…"

In the end, her mother decided to copy out the phone book.

Writing books that were intended for the library of rejects was a far cry from the original project, but Magali didn't care; the eight books that she collected within the space of a few days made Jean-Pierre very happy. He saw it as a stirring of hope, a sign that all was not lost. He knew he wouldn't be able to witness the library's recovery for much longer, so he made Magali promise that she would at least keep all the rejected books they had accumulated up to now.

"I promise, Jean-Pierre."

"Those writers put their trust in us… We can't betray them."

"I'll look after them. They'll be protected here. And there will always be a place for books that nobody wants."

"Thank you."

"Jean-Pierre…"

"Yes?"

"I wanted to thank you…"

"For what?"

"For giving me *The Lover*… It's such a beautiful book."

"…"

He took Magali's hand and held it for a long time. A few minutes later, alone in her car, she started to cry.

*

The following week, Jean-Pierre Gourvec died in his bed. People talked about him as a lovable man who would be missed by everyone. But very few mourners attended the brief ceremony at the cemetery. What would remain of this man, in the end? On the day of his funeral, it was perhaps possible to understand his determination to create and expand the library of rejected books. It was a sort of gravestone, a bulwark against oblivion. Nobody came to lay flowers at his graveside, just as nobody came to read the rejected books.

*

Of course Magali kept her promise to look after the books they'd already acquired, but she had no time to seek out new ones. For the last few months, the local government had been trying to cut spending, particularly on anything cultural. After Gourvec's death, while Magali took over the running of the library, she was not allowed to hire an assistant. She found herself alone. Gradually, the shelves at the back of the library would be abandoned, and dust would cover those unread words. Magali was so busy carrying out more pressing tasks that she rarely spared a thought for the rejects. How could she possibly imagine that they would one day turn her whole life upside down?

PART TWO

I

D ELPHINE DESPERO had lived in Paris for almost ten years, kept there by work commitments, but she had never lost her attachment to Brittany. She appeared taller than she actually was, and the illusion had nothing to do with high heels. It's difficult to explain how some people manage to grow in this way: is it ambition, the fact of having been loved as a child, the certainty of a radiant future? Maybe a little of all of this. Delphine was the kind of woman you wanted to listen to, to follow; she had a kind of gentle charisma. Her mother was a literature teacher, and she was born among words. She spent her childhood examining the essays written by her mother's students, fascinated by the red ink of correction; she scrutinized their mistakes, their awkward sentences, memorizing all the things she shouldn't do.

When she finished secondary school, she went to the University of Rennes to study literature, but she had no desire to become a teacher. Her dream was to work in publishing. She spent her summers doing internships or any work that would allow her to enter the literary world. She had realized very early in life that she didn't feel capable of being a writer; she was not frustrated by this, but more than anything she wanted to work with writers. She would never forget the frisson she felt the first time she saw Michel Houellebecq. At the time, she'd been an intern at Éditions Fayard, who had published *The Possibility of an Island*. He had paused for a moment in front of her, not really to look at her, but rather, let's say, to sniff her. She had stammered *hello* and received no response, and to her this seemed the most extraordinary conversation of her life.

The following weekend, back at her parents' house, she'd spoken about that moment for more than an hour. She admired Houellebecq and *his incredible novelistic sensibility*. She was bored by all the controversies surrounding him; nobody ever paid enough attention to his language, his despair, his humour. She talked about him as though they were old friends, as if the simple fact of having passed him in a corridor enabled her to understand his work better than anyone else. She was in a state of exaltation, and her parents watched her with amusement; they'd done everything they could, when educating their daughter, to fill her with enthusiasm, fascination, wonder; in this sense, they had clearly succeeded. Delphine had developed an ability to sense the interior drives that gave life to a narrative. Everyone who met her during this period agreed that she had a promising future.

After an internship at Grasset, she was hired as a junior editor. She was exceptionally young for such a position, but all success is the fruit of good timing; she had appeared in the publishing house at a time when the management wished to make the editorial team younger and more female. She was given a few authors—not the most prestigious, it has to be said, but they were all happy to have a young editor who would devote all her time and energy to them. She was also expected to look at the unsolicited manuscripts they received whenever she had some spare time. She was the one who discovered Laurent Binet's extraordinary first novel, *HHhH*. As soon as she finished it, she hurried to see Olivier Nora, the CEO of Grasset, and urged him to read it as soon as possible. Her enthusiasm was rewarded. Binet signed with Grasset just before Gallimard offered him a contract. A few months later, the book won the Prix Goncourt for a First Novel, and Delphine Despero was given a promotion.

2

A few weeks after that, she was filled once again with a rush of enthusiasm when she read the first novel by a young author named Frédéric Koskas. *The Bathtub* was about a teenage boy who refused to leave the bathroom and decided to live inside the bathtub. The story was written in prose that was simultaneously joyous and melancholic, and Delphine had never read anything like it. She had no trouble convincing the reading committee to follow her advice by making an offer for the book. She was reminded of Goncharov's *Oblomov* and Calvino's *Baron in the Trees*, but there was also a contemporary dimension to the theme of the protagonist's rejection of the world. The biggest difference was that, thanks to the internet, twenty-four-hour news, social media and so on, every adolescent in the world could potentially know everything there was to know about life… so why bother leaving the house? Delphine was capable of talking about this novel for hours on end. She immediately considered Koskas to be a genius. Despite her easily aroused excitement, this was a word that she used only rarely. However, we should bear in mind one additional detail: she had fallen head over heels in love with the author of *The Bathtub*.

They met several times before the signing of the contract: first, in the offices of Grasset, then in a café, and lastly at the bar of a posh hotel. They spoke about the novel together, and about how it would be published. Koskas's heart pounded at the thought that he would soon have a novel in print; this was his ultimate dream, his name on the cover of a book. He felt certain now that his life was about to begin. With his name on a novel, he had always imagined that he would become a floating being, torn free of all roots. He told Delphine about his influences, and they chatted about their favourite authors—she was very well read—but never did their conversation drift into the realms of intimacy. The young editor was dying to know if her new author had a girlfriend, but she never allowed herself to ask him that question. She tried to find out through more indirect means, but in vain. In the end it was Frédéric who made the first move.

"May I ask you something personal?"

"Yes, of course."

"Do you have a boyfriend?"

"You want me to be honest?"

"Yes."

"I don't have a boyfriend."

"How is that possible?"

"Because I was waiting for you," Delphine replied, surprising herself with her spontaneity.

She wanted to take the words back as soon as they were out of her mouth, to say that she was just kidding, but she knew perfectly well how sincere she had sounded. Of course, Frédéric had played his own part in this dialogue of seduction by asking her "How is that possible?" Clearly that implied that he liked her, didn't it? She sat there blushing, while gradually admitting to herself that her words had been dictated by her true feelings—feelings that were pure, and therefore uncontrollable. Yes, she had always wanted a man like him. Physically and intellectually. It's sometimes said that love at first sight is actually the recognition of a desire that has always existed inside us. From their first meeting, Delphine had felt this—the sensation that she already knew this man, that she had perhaps glimpsed him in premonitory dreams.

Frédéric, taken by surprise, didn't know what to say. To him, Delphine had seemed *completely* sincere. When she praised his novel, he could always detect a hint of hyperbole. A sort of professional obligation to appear upbeat, he imagined. But here, the tone was bereft of irony or exaggeration; her meaning could only be taken at face value. He had to say something, and the future of their relationship hung on the words he chose. Wouldn't he prefer to keep her at a distance? To concentrate uniquely on interactions related to his novel, and the ones he would write in the future? But there was already a connection.

He could not be indifferent to this woman who understood him so well, this woman who had changed his life. Lost in the labyrinth of his thoughts, he forced Delphine to speak again:

"If my attraction for you isn't reciprocated, I will of course publish your novel with the same enthusiasm."

"Thank you for clarifying that."

"You're welcome."

"So, let's say we were together…" said Frédéric in a suddenly amused tone of voice.

"Yes, let's say we were…"

"If we ever split up, what would happen?"

"Wow, you're really pessimistic. Nothing has even started yet, and you're already talking about it ending."

"I'd like an answer, though: if one day you end up hating me, will you have all the copies of my book pulped?"

"Well, yes, obviously. That's just a risk you'll have to take."

"…"

He stared at her, and started to smile, and that was how it all began.

3

They left the bar and went for a walk through the streets of Paris. They became tourists in their own city, wandering around aimlessly before arriving at Delphine's apartment. She rented a bedsit near Montmartre, a neighbourhood that can't decide if it's working class or bourgeois. They climbed the stairs leading to the second floor: a sort of foreplay. Frédéric watched Delphine's legs, which, aware of being observed, advanced slowly. Once inside the apartment, they headed to the bed and lay down without any frenzy; sometimes, the most intense desire can lead to a calmness that is just as exciting. Soon after that, they made love. And remained in each other's arms for a long time, the two of them struck by the wonderful weirdness of being suddenly and completely intimate with somebody who, a few hours before, had still been a stranger. The transformation was rapid, it was glorious. Delphine's body had found the destination it had sought for so long. Frédéric felt finally at peace; a void that he hadn't even realized was inside him had been filled. And they both knew that what they'd experienced simply never happened. Or only to other people.

In the middle of the night, Delphine turned on the light.

"It's time to talk about your contract."

"Ah… so this was a negotiating tactic…"

"Naturally. I sleep with all my authors before signing. It makes it easier to retain audiovisual rights."

"…"

"So?"

"You can have them. You can have all my rights."

4

Unfortunately, *The Bathtub* was a failure. And yet "failure" is perhaps an overstatement. What can anyone expect from the publication of a novel? Despite all Delphine Despero's efforts, despite all her contacts in the press, despite several reviews praising *the inspired storytelling of this promising talent*, Frédéric's novel suffered the classic destiny of most published novels. When you are unpublished, you believe that the holy grail is publication. But there is a fate worse than the pain of not being published: being published in complete obscurity.[3] After only a few days, your book is nowhere to be seen, and you find yourself somewhat pathetically wandering from one bookshop to the next in search of some proof that it wasn't all a dream. Publishing a novel that nobody reads is like encountering the world's indifference *in person*.

Delphine did her best to reassure Frédéric, telling him that this setback had not diminished Grasset's faith in him. But nothing worked: he felt empty and humiliated. He had lived for years with the certainty that one day he would exist through words. He had enjoyed the image of being a young man who writes and who, soon, will have a first novel published. But what could he hope for now that reality had dressed his dream in rags? He had no desire to play-act, to go into false ecstasies over the critical acclaim his novel had received, like so many others who boast about a three-line mention in *Le Monde*. Frédéric Koskas had always viewed his situation objectively. And he realized that he shouldn't change what was now his defining characteristic. People didn't read him; that's just how

3   Richard Brautigan could have created another library, for published books about which nobody says a word: *the library of invisible books*.

it was. "At least I met the woman I love through publishing this novel," he thought consolingly. He had to keep going, with the conviction of a soldier who's been left behind by his regiment. A few weeks later, he started writing again. A novel with the provisional title of *The Bed*. He didn't tell Delphine what the book was about. All he said was: "If it's going to be another failure, it may as well be more comfortable than a bathtub."

5

They moved in together. In other words, Frédéric moved his stuff to Delphine's apartment. To protect their love from gossip, they kept it a secret within the publishing house. In the morning, she went off to work and he sat down to write. He had decided to write this new book entirely in their bed. Writing provides you with some extraordinary alibis. Writing is the only job in the world where you can stay under the duvet all day long and still claim to be working. Sometimes he fell back asleep or daydreamed, persuading himself that it was useful for his creativity. The reality, however, was that his creativity was all dried up. It occurred to him that this lovely, comfortable happiness that had fallen from the sky might actually be damaging his ability to write. Did you have to be lost or fragile in order to create? No, that was absurd. Masterpieces had been written amid euphoria and masterpieces had been written amid despair. In fact, for the first time in his life, there was a support structure to his existence. And Delphine could earn enough money for both of them while he wrote his book. He didn't think of himself as a parasite or a helpless person, but he'd accepted the idea of being kept. It was a sort of lovers' pact: he was working for her, after all, because she would publish his novel. But he also knew that she would judge the book impartially, that her love for him would have no effect on her opinion of the novel's quality.

In the meantime, she was publishing other authors, and her reputation as an editor continued to grow. She turned down several offers from other publishers because she felt profoundly attached to Grasset, the company that had given her the big break she'd craved. Occasionally Frédéric would get jealous. "Oh really? You published this book? But why? It's so bad." She replied: "Don't become one of those embittered authors who finds all other books unreadable. I have to deal with too many egotistical bores all day. When I get home, I want to see an author focused entirely on his work. The others don't matter. Besides, I'm just publishing them while I wait for your *bed*. Everything I do in life is basically waiting for your bed." Delphine had a brilliant knack for defusing Frédéric's anxieties. She was a perfect mix of a literary dreamer and a pragmatic woman; she drew her strength from her origins, and from the love of her parents.

6

Ah yes, her parents. Delphine talked to her mother on the phone every day, recounting her life in minute detail. She talked to

34

her father too, but the version she gave him was more succinct. The two of them were both recently retired. "I was raised by a French teacher and a maths teacher, which explains my schizophrenia," Delphine would joke. Her father had taught in Brest, and her mother in Quimper, and every evening they would return to their home in the village of Morgat, near Crozon. It was a magical place, a refuge, dominated by the wildness of nature. It was impossible to be bored in a place like that; you could fill a whole life with contemplation of the sea.

Delphine spent all her summer holidays at her parents' house, and this one was no exception to that rule. She asked Frédéric to come with her. It would be an opportunity for him to finally meet Fabienne and Gérard. He pretended to hesitate, as if he might have something better to do. He asked her: "What's your bed like?"

"Unsullied by any man."

"So I'd be the first to sleep with you there?"

"The first—and the last, I hope."

"I wish I could write the way you answer my questions. What you say is always so beautiful, powerful, precise."

"You write better than that. I know that better than anyone."

"You're wonderful."

"You're not bad yourself."

" . . . "

"It's the end of the world, where my parents live. We'll go for walks by the sea, and everything will be clear."

"And your parents? I'm not always very sociable when I'm writing."

35

"They'll understand. We talk all the time, but we don't expect anyone else to do the same. That's Brittany."

"What does that mean, 'That's Brittany'? You say that all the time."

"You'll see."

"…"

7

Things didn't go quite like that. As soon as they arrived in the house, Frédéric felt warmly devoured by Delphine's parents. He was the first boyfriend she'd ever introduced to them; that was obvious. They wanted to know everything. So much for the supposed non-obligation to talk. He was uncomfortable with the idea of digging up the past, but they immediately interrogated him about his life, his parents, his childhood. He tried to throw them tokens of sociability, sprinkling his answers with charming anecdotes. Delphine had the feeling that he was inventing these stories to make his life sound more thrilling than the bleak reality. She was right.

Gérard had read *The Bathtub*. It is always slightly depressing for an author who has published an unsuccessful book to meet a reader who tries to make them feel better by talking about it interminably. Of course, the intention is a good one. But, barely had they arrived, drinking the first aperitif on the terrace, overlooking that breathtakingly beautiful landscape, than Frédéric felt embarrassed that the moment should be encumbered by a conversation about his novel, which was, he thought, ultimately pretty mediocre. Gradually, he was beginning to detach himself from it, to perceive its faults, its try-hard prose. As if every sentence had to provide immediate proof of its author's brilliance. A first novel is always a bit of a teacher's pet. Only geniuses can instantly produce dunces. But it undoubtedly takes time to understand how to let a story breathe, how to create something behind the shows of brilliance. Frédéric had the feeling that his second novel would be better; he thought this constantly without ever mentioning it to anyone. He didn't want to spread his intuitions too thin by sharing them.

"*The Bathtub* is an excellent parable of contemporary life," Gérard went on.

"Ah…" replied Frédéric.

"You're right: profusion created confusion, to start with. And now it is producing a desire for renunciation. If everything is of equal value then nothing means anything. A very pertinent equation, in my opinion."

"Thank you. You're making me blush with all these compliments…"

"Better enjoy them. It's not normally like that around here," he said, laughing a little too heartily.

"I sensed the influence of Robert Walser. Am I right?" Fabienne asked.

"Robert Walser… I… yes… it's true, I like his work a lot. I hadn't thought about him as an influence, but you're probably right."

"Your novel reminded me most of all of his short story, 'The Promenade'. He has an incredible talent for evoking the act of walking. Swiss authors are often the best when it comes to boredom and solitude. There's some of that in your novel: you make emptiness fascinating."

Frédéric was speechless; he felt choked by emotion. When had he last felt such kindliness, such attention? In a few phrases, they had bandaged the wounds left by the public's incomprehension. He looked at Delphine, who had changed his life, and she smiled at him very tenderly. He thought how eager he was to discover that famous bed where no man had been before him. Here, their love seemed to have ascended to a higher plane.

8

After this chatty introduction, Delphine's parents didn't ask Frédéric too many questions. The days passed, and he took great pleasure in writing and in exploring this region that was, for him, unknown. He wrote in the mornings, and in the afternoons he went walking with Delphine, roaming the countryside and never meeting anyone. It was the ideal setting in which to forget himself. Here and there, she would tell him anecdotes about her adolescence. The past came together bit by bit, and now Frédéric was able to love every era of Delphine's life.

Delphine used her spare time to catch up with childhood friends. This is a particular category of friendship: affinities are, above all, geographical. In Paris, she would perhaps have nothing to say to Pierrick or Sophie, since they had become so different, but here they could talk for hours. They each recounted their life, year after year. The other two asked Delphine about the celebrities she'd met. "There are lots of superficial people," she said, without really believing it. So often, we tell people what we think they want to hear. Delphine knew that her childhood friends wanted to hear her criticize Paris; it reassured them. Time passed pleasantly with them, but she was always eager to get back to Frédéric. She was happy that he felt at ease writing in Brittany. She recommended his novel to her friends, and they asked if it was out in paperback. She had to admit that it wasn't. Despite her growing influence as an editor, she had not been able to convince anyone to publish a mass-market edition of a book that had flopped so completely. There was no objective reason to believe that a cheaper price would alter the commercial fate of *The Bathtub*.

Delphine preferred to change the subject, so she told them about the novels she'd brought with her. With the advent of new technologies, there was no longer any need to lug manuscripts around in her suitcases during the holidays. She had about twenty books to read during August, and they were all stored on her e-reader. They asked her what those novels were about, and Delphine confessed that, most of the time, she was incapable of summarizing them. She had not read anything memorable. Yet she continued to feel excited at the start of each new book. Because what if it was good? What if she was about to discover a new author? She found her job so stimulating, it was almost like being a child again, hunting for chocolate eggs in a garden at Easter. And she adored working on the manuscripts of the authors she published. She had reread *The Bathtub* at least ten times. When she loved a novel, the choice of keeping or deleting a comma could make her heart beat faster.

9

The weather was so beautiful that evening that they decided to eat dinner outside. Frédéric set the table, and took a slightly ridiculous pleasure in feeling useful. Writers are so happy at the idea of performing a household chore. They like to counterbalance their airy wanderings with something concrete. Delphine talked a lot with her parents, which fascinated her boyfriend. They always have something to say to one another, he thought; there was never a blank page in their conversation. Perhaps it was a question of momentum: one word led to another. Watching them and listening to them made Frédéric even more acutely aware of his inability to communicate with his own parents. Had they even read his novel? Probably not. His mother tried to act more tenderly towards him, but it was difficult to fill the void of all those years of emotional drought. Anyway, he rarely thought about them. When was the last time they had talked? He really couldn't remember. The failure of his novel had rendered them even more distant. He didn't want to see that look of contempt in his father's eyes as he talked about all those other novels that had been successful.

Frédéric didn't even know what they were doing that summer. He found it strange enough that they should be together at all. After twenty years of separation, his parents had become a couple again. What were they thinking? It was probably a good reason to become a novelist: the inability to understand your own parents. He imagined that they had sampled life without each other and, for want of anything better, had decided to get back together. Frédéric had suffered, as a child, from the need to constantly shuttle his belongings from one home to another, and now they'd decided to become a family again, without him. Was he supposed to feel guilty? The truth was probably much simpler: they were terrified by loneliness.

Frédéric abandoned these thoughts[4] and returned to the present:

"Don't you get sick of reading all those manuscripts?" Fabienne asked her daughter.

"No, I adore it! Although recently, I must admit, I've got a bit tired of it. I haven't read anything very exciting."

"And *The Bathtub*? How did you discover that?"

4 How long had he tuned out of the conversation? Impossible to say. A human being is endowed with this unique capacity to nod and give the illusion of listening attentively, all the while thinking about something else completely. That is why we should never hope to read the truth in somebody else's expression.

"Frédéric sent it in the post. And I spotted it while I was rummaging through all the manuscripts on the desk. I was drawn by the title."

"Actually, I left it at the reception desk," said Frédéric. "I went to several different publishing houses, without really believing it would come to anything. I certainly never imagined I'd get a call the next morning!"

"I imagine it must be rare for it to happen so quickly?" said Gérard, always keen to participate in a conversation, even if the subject didn't really interest him.

"The speed is rare, yes. But even acceptance is rare. At Grasset, we only publish about three or four unsolicited novels each year."

"Out of how many?"

"Thousands."

"I suppose somebody must be employed to reject all the others," said Gérard. "What a job…"

"It's generally just a standard rejection letter, sent by an intern," Delphine explained.

"Ah yes, the famous letter: 'Despite the many qualities of your work, blah-blah-blah… we regret to inform you that it does not meet our editorial criteria… Yours sincerely blah-blah-blah…' It's always the fault of the editorial criteria!"

"You're right," Delphine replied to her mother. "Particularly as the editorial criteria don't even exist—that's just a pretext. Just leaf through our catalogue and you'd see that the books we publish are all completely different."

There was a brief lull in the conversation then, a rarity in the Despero family. Gérard took advantage of this to pour everyone another glass of red. They had already got through three bottles that evening.

Fabienne filled the silence with a local anecdote:

"A few years ago, the librarian in Crozon got it into his head to start collecting all the books rejected by publishers."

"Really?" said Delphine, surprised that she didn't know this story.

"Oh yes. The project was inspired by an American library, I believe. I'm not too sure of the details now. I just remember that it caused quite a stir at the time. People found it amusing. Someone even said that it was a sort of literary rubbish tip."

"That's stupid. I think it's a good idea," Frédéric interjected. "If nobody had wanted my book, I'd have liked it to be accepted somewhere."

"Does it still exist?" asked Delphine.

"Yes. I don't think it's very active any more, but I went to the library a few months ago and I noticed that all the shelves at the back were still filled with rejected books."

"There must be some real duds in there!" laughed Gérard, but nobody seemed to appreciate his sense of humour.

Frédéric realized that Delphine's father must often have been sidelined by the two women in the family. Out of sympathy, he shot him a brief complicit smile, but he didn't actually laugh. Gérard became serious again, and acknowledged that he found the whole concept absurd. As a mathematician, he could not imagine that there existed a place devoted to all the unfinished scientific research projects or all the failed exams.

43

The whole point was that there were measures of validity, barriers that had to be passed, to demarcate the boundaries between the worlds of success and failure. He came up with another comparison, a strange one to say the least: "It's like, in love, if a woman said no to you, but you were allowed to have an affair with her anyway…" Delphine and Fabienne did not understand this analogy, but condescendingly praised this pathetic attempt by a rational man to show his tender side. Scientists do sometimes come up with these poetic metaphors, they said, about as subtle as a poem written by a four-year-old. (It was time for bed.)

10

In the privacy of their room, Frédéric caressed Delphine's calves, then her thighs, then stopped with his finger in one particular spot.

"And if I put this here, will you refuse?" he whispered.

11

The next morning, Delphine suggested to Frédéric that they ride their bikes to Crozon, to take a look at that library. He usually worked until at least one in the afternoon, but he too felt a pressing desire to go. It would perhaps do him good to witness a physical manifestation of others' failure.

Magali still worked at the library. She'd put on weight. Without really knowing why, she had let herself go. It hadn't started straight after the birth of her two sons, but a few years later. Perhaps at the moment when she realized that she would live her whole life here, and that she would stay in the same job until retirement. This solid horizon put a sudden end to her interest in her looks. And when she noticed that her extra pounds didn't really bother her husband either, she continued along a path that led to her no longer recognizing herself. Her husband told her that he loved her despite her physical changes; she might have taken this as proof of the depth of his love, but instead she saw it as proof of indifference.

Another important change should be noted in Magali: year by year, she had become literary. She had become a librarian by chance, without any real taste for books, but now she was capable of advising readers, guiding them in their choices. The library had gradually evolved in her image. She had created a bigger children's section, with special events where people would read books out loud. Her sons, now adults, would sometimes come to give her a hand at the weekends. They were giants now and, like their father, they worked at the Renault garage, but still you would sometimes find them squeezed into the children's section, reading *The Story of the Little Mole Who Went in Search of Whodunit* to a bunch of kids.

Very few people came these days to visit the library of rejects, and Magali had almost forgotten about it herself. Sometimes, a rather shady individual would enter shyly and mutter that nobody had wanted his book. He'd heard about this refuge from his unpublished writer friends. The word was passed along through this community of disillusion.

The young couple went into the library, and Delphine introduced herself, explaining that she lived in Morgat.

"Oh, you're the Desperos' daughter?" Magali asked.

"Yes."

"I remember you. You used to come here when you were little."

"That's right."

"Well, it was mostly your mother who came to borrow books for you. But aren't you the one who works in Paris for a publishing company?"

"Yes, that's me."

"Do you think you'd be able to let us have some free books?" asked Magali, whose commercial acumen was considerably stronger than her tactfulness.

"Um… yes, of course. I'll see what I can do."

"Thank you."

"Anyway, I can recommend a very good novel to you. *The Bathtub*. I could probably get you a few free copies of that."

"Oh yes, I heard about that. Apparently it's rubbish."

"That's not true at all. In fact, allow me to introduce its author…"

"Oh, I'm sorry. Me and my big mouth!"

"Don't worry about it," Frédéric reassured her. "I'm just as bad. I often say that a book's supposed to be rubbish, without having read it."

46

"But I am going to read it now. And put it on display. After all, it's not every day that a star comes to Crozon!"

"Well, I'm not really a star," Frédéric stammered.

"Well, you know what I mean. A published author."

"Talking of which…" said Delphine. "We came to see you because we heard about a slightly odd kind of library."

"Ah, I imagine you're talking about the rejected books."

"Exactly."

"It's over there, at the back. I kept it as a tribute to its founder, but it's probably full of really bad books."

"Yes, probably," said Delphine. "But we adore the idea."

"Gourvec would be so pleased. He was the man who created it. He liked it when people took an interest in his library. It was his life's work, if you like. He made others' failures his own success."

"That's very beautiful," Frédéric said.

Magali had uttered that phrase spontaneously, without realizing its poetry. She watched as the young couple moved towards the shelves of rejected books and thought about how long it was since she'd dusted that part of the library.

PART THREE

I

A FEW DAYS LATER, Delphine and Frédéric returned to the library. It had enchanted them, reading all those improbable stories. There had been a few fits of hysterical giggling as they read out the titles, but they had also been moved by some of the personal diary entries; they may have been badly written, but there was a trueness of feeling to them all the same.

They spent a whole afternoon there, unaware of time passing. In the evening, Delphine's mother stood in the garden anxiously awaiting their return. She finally saw them, just before sunset. They appeared in the distance, preceded by the lights on their bicycles. She immediately recognized her daughter from the precise, unswerving way she rode a bike. Her arrival was heralded by that straight, mechanical ray of light. Frédéric's was more artistic, advancing in fits and starts, drifting from side to side. You could imagine him constantly looking around. They made a good couple, Fabienne thought then: an alliance of the concrete and the dreamy.

"Sorry, Mama, my phone battery died. And we were delayed."

"By what?"

"By something amazing."

"What happened?"

"First call Papa. Everybody must be here for this."

She pronounced this last phrase in a solemn voice.

2

A few minutes later, over aperitifs, Delphine and Frédéric told her parents about their afternoon in the library. They took turns to speak, one telling an anecdote while the other clarified certain details. You could tell that they wanted to make the moment last, that they didn't want to reveal the momentous news too quickly. They talked about how they'd laughed at some of the manuscripts, particularly the more bizarre and obscene ones such as *Masturbation and Sushi*, an erotic ode to raw fish. The parents begged them to get to the point, but it made no difference; they wanted to take the scenic route, stop a few times to contemplate the landscape, turning their account of the afternoon into a slow, delicious adventure. Until the punchline:

"And then we found a masterpiece," Delphine announced.

"Oh?"

"To start with, I thought there were a few good pages—I mean, why not, after all?—and then I was just swept away by the story. I couldn't put that book down. I read the whole thing in two hours. It blew me away. And it was written in such a strange style, simple and poetic at the same time. As soon as I finished it, I gave it to Frédéric to read, and… I've never seen him like that before. He looked completely captivated."

"Yes, it's true," Frédéric confirmed. He appeared to be still in a state of shock.

"But what's it about, this book?"

"We borrowed the manuscript—you can read it."

"You just took it?"

"Yes. I don't think anyone will mind."

"So what's the subject?"

"It's called *The Last Hours of a Love Affair*. It's magnificent. It's about a passion that has to end. For various reasons, the couple can't love each other any more. The book recounts their final moments. But what makes the book so unique is that, in parallel with this, the author describes the death of Pushkin."

"Yes, Pushkin was wounded in a duel," Frédéric went on. "He was in agony for hours before he finally died. It's an extraordinary idea to blend the end of a love affair with the death throes of a great Russian poet."

"And the book begins with the sentence: 'One cannot understand Russia if one has not read Pushkin'," Delphine added.

"I can't wait to read it," said Gérard.

"You? I thought you didn't like reading," said Fabienne.

"Yes, but this makes me want to."

Delphine observed her father. Not as his daughter, but as an editor. She immediately realized that this novel could move readers. And, of course, the way it had been discovered would make for a great story.

"Who's the author?" the mother asked.

"I don't know. His name is Henri Pick. On the manu-script, it says that he lives in Crozon. Should be easy enough to find…"

"Hmm, that name is familiar," said the father. "In fact, isn't it the guy who ran the pizzeria for a long time?"

The young couple stared at Gérard. He was not the kind of man who made mistakes. It seemed improbable, but then the whole adventure had been improbable.

By the next morning, Delphine's mother had read the book too. She had found the story beautiful, and quite simple. "And it's true that there's a sort of tragic power that emanates from the parallel with Pushkin's death," she added. "I didn't know about that before I read the book."

"Pushkin isn't very famous in France," Delphine replied.

"His death is so absurd…"

Fabienne wanted to talk more about the Russian poet and how he died, but Delphine interrupted her to talk about the book's author. She'd spent all night thinking about it. Who could have written a book like that without becoming well known?

It wasn't too difficult to find information about the mystery man. Frédéric typed his name into Google and discovered an obituary from two years before. So Henri Pick would never know that his book had found enthusiastic readers, including an editor. Delphine decided that they should meet his family. The obituary had mentioned a wife and daughter. The widow lived in Crozon, and her address was in the phone book. It was hardly an investigation worthy of a thriller.

3

Madeleine Pick had just turned eighty and had lived alone since her husband's death. For more than forty years, they had run the pizzeria together. Henri worked in the kitchen, and she was the waitress. Their entire life had fitted around the rhythms of the restaurant. They didn't want to retire, because it would have been a terrible wrench. But Henri's body could no longer take the pace. He suffered a heart attack and, reluctantly, decided to sell the pizzeria. Sometimes he would go back there as a customer. He admitted to Madeleine that eating there was like watching an old flame with her new husband. In his final years, he became increasingly morose, detached from everything, with no appetite for life. His wife, who had always been the more cheerful, outgoing one, watched helplessly as he sank into depression. He died in his bed, a few days after walking for too long in the rain; it was hard to say if that had been a form of suicide disguised as carelessness. On his deathbed, he had appeared serene. Now Madeleine spent most of her days alone, but she never got bored. Sometimes she would do embroidery— a ridiculous pastime in her opinion, but one for which she had developed a taste. As she was finishing the last rows of a doily, the doorbell rang.

She opened it without fear, which surprised Frédéric. This region seemed free of all apprehension regarding strangers.

"Hello. We're sorry to disturb you, but… are you Madame Pick?"

"Yes, until proven otherwise, that's me."

"And your husband's name was Henri?"

"Until he died, that was his name."

"My name is Delphine Despero. I'm not sure if you know my parents. They're from Morgat."

"Yes, maybe. I saw so many people, with the restaurant. But that name rings a bell. Did you have pigtails and a red bike when you were a little girl?"

Delphine was speechless. How could this woman remember such details? But yes, that was her. For a brief instant, she felt again the sensation of being a little girl, pigtails flying in the wind as she rode her red bicycle.

They went into the living room. The silence was disturbed by a clock that reminded everyone of its presence by ticking very loudly. Madeleine must have stopped hearing it. The noise of each second had become her regular sonic backdrop. The knick-knacks scattered all over the room gave it the appearance of a Breton souvenir shop. Nobody could have been in any doubt about the house's geographical setting: it oozed Brittany, and there was no trace of any trips to other places. When Delphine asked the old woman if she sometimes went to Paris, the response was scathing: "I went there once. What a nightmare! The crowds, the stress, the smell. And, honestly, the Eiffel Tower? I can't see what all the fuss is about!"

"..."

"Can I offer you something to drink?"

"Oh, yes please."

"What would you like?"

"Whatever you're having," said Delphine, who had realized it was better not to rush things. The old woman went into the kitchen, leaving her guests in the living room. Delphine and Frédéric glanced at each other in an awkward silence. Madeleine quickly returned with two cups of caramel tea.

Out of politeness, Frédéric drank his tea, even though he loathed the smell of caramel more than anything. He did not feel at ease in this house; the atmosphere was oppressive, even a little scary. He had the feeling that terrible things had happened here. Then he spotted a photograph on the mantelpiece. The portrait of a gruff-looking man, with a thick moustache.

"Is that your husband?" he asked in a low voice.

"Yes. It's one of my favourite pictures of him. He looks happy in that one. And he's smiling, which was quite rare. Henri was not the sociable type."

"..."

This reply seemed to offer a concrete dimension to the theory of relativity: the young couple could not discern even the hint of a smile in that photograph, and certainly no sign of happiness. On the contrary, Henri's expression seemed to communicate a deep sadness. Yet Madeleine kept going on about the feeling of *joie de vivre* that emanated from the portrait.

Delphine didn't want to rush her hostess. It was better to let her talk for a while, about her life, her husband, before she brought up the reason for their visit. Madeleine spoke about her old job, the hours that Henri spent at the restaurant

57

preparing everything. There's not much to tell, she admitted in the end. *The time passed so quickly*, and here we are. Until this moment, she had seemed detached as she reminisced about the past, but suddenly she was choked by emotion. She realized that she never talked to anybody about Henri. Since his death, he had disappeared from conversations, from daily life, perhaps even from the memories of everyone who'd known him. And so she started confiding secrets, which was out of character, without even wondering why these two strangers sitting in her living room wanted to hear her talk about her deceased husband. When an event occurs that gives you a sense of well-being, you tend not to question its cause. Little by little, Delphine and Frédéric formed an impression of a man whose life had been utterly discreet and free of drama.

"Did he have any passions?" Delphine asked eventually, in an attempt to accelerate the conversation.

"…"

"Did you have a typewriter at the pizzeria?"

"What? A typewriter?"

"Yes."

"No. Never."

"Did he like to read?" asked Delphine.

"Read? Henri?" the old woman asked with a smile. "No, I never saw him read a book. Apart from the TV guide, he never read anything at all."

The faces of the two visitors expressed a mixture of stupefaction and excitement. Confronted by their silence, Madeleine abruptly added: "Actually, I've just thought of something. When we sold the pizzeria, we spent days on end packing all our stuff. All the things we'd accumulated over the years. And I remember finding a cardboard box in the cellar, full of books."

"So you think he might have been reading at the restaurant, without you knowing?"

"No. I asked him what they were, and he told me they were all the books left behind by our customers over the years. He'd put them there in case they came back to claim them. It struck me as a bit strange, because I couldn't remember any customers leaving books on the tables. But I wasn't there all the time. And when the shift was over, I often went back home while he cleaned up. He was in the pizzeria much more than I was. He'd get there at eight or nine in the morning, and come home at midnight."

"Oh yeah, that's a long day," observed Frédéric.

"Henri liked it that way. He adored the mornings, when there was nobody to bother him. He'd prepare his dough, and sometimes he'd change the menu so people didn't get bored. He enjoyed inventing new pizzas, and coming up with names for them. I remember the Brigitte Bardot... and the Stalin, with its red chilli peppers."

"Why Stalin?"

"Oh, I don't know. He had these fancies sometimes. He liked Russia. Well, he liked Russians anyway. He said they were a proud people, a bit like the Bretons."

"..."

"Excuse me, but I have to visit a friend at the hospital. Those are my only outings these days—the hospital, the retirement home and the cemetery. The magic trio. But why did you want to see me?"

"Do you have to leave now?"

"Yes."

"In that case," said Delphine, disappointed, "the best thing would be to meet again later, because what we have to tell you might take a while."

"Ah… that sounds intriguing. But I really do have to go."

"Thank you for taking the time to see us."

"You're welcome. Did you like the caramel tea?"

"Yes, thank you," chorused Delphine and Frédéric.

"Oh good, because someone gave it to me, and I don't like the taste at all. So I try to get rid of it when I have guests."

The two Parisians gaped at her, and Madeleine added that she was just kidding. As she got older, she had come to realize that nobody imagined she was capable of having a sense of humour. Old people, it was assumed, were gloomy sods, incapable of sarcasm, who didn't understand anything.

As they were leaving, Delphine asked Madeleine when they might see her again. With an ironic smile, the old woman replied that she had plenty of free time. So, whenever they wanted. They agreed to meet up the next day. The old lady moved closer to Frédéric and said: "You don't look well."

"Oh?"

"You should take more walks by the sea."

"You're right. I don't get out enough."

"What do you do?"

"I write."

She gave him a look of dismay.

4

When she saw her friend in the hospital, Madeleine told her about the visit she'd just had. To entertain the patient, she lingered on the story of the caramel tea. Sylviane squeezed her hand, a sign that she'd enjoyed the anecdote. The two women had known each other since childhood: they'd skipped rope in the playground together, they'd told each other about their first time with a boy, they'd conversed about their children's problems at school, and life had gone on like that until their husbands had died at almost exactly the same time. And now one of them was going to leave before the other.

5

After that curtailed visit, Delphine and Frédéric decided to eat lunch in the restaurant that used to belong to the Picks. The pizzeria had become a crêperie, which seemed more logical. People visited Brittany to eat crêpes and drink cider. You had to submit to the culinary diktat of each region. With the arrival of the new owners, the restaurant's clientele had radically changed; the local regulars had given way to tourists.

They looked around the premises to familiarize themselves with the idea that Pick had written his novel here. To Frédéric, it seemed unlikely: "It's charmless, hot, noisy… Can you really imagine him writing here?"

"Yes. In winter, there's nobody here. It's hard to believe, but for many months of the year it's very quiet. The perfect depressing atmosphere that writers need."

"True. That's exactly what I think when I'm writing in your place: the perfect depressing atmosphere."

"Very funny…"

They were both cheerful, and increasingly excited by this whole story. They'd been impressed by Madeleine's personality. They were eager to see her reaction, the next day, when she learnt about her husband's secret.

The waitress[5] asked them what they wanted. As always, Delphine made her choice quickly (in this case, a seafood salad) while Frédéric hesitated for minutes on end, his eyes frantically roaming the menu, like a writer struggling with an ill-formed sentence. In search of a solution to his dilemma, he looked around him at the plates on other people's tables. The crêpes looked good, but which one should he choose? He weighed up the pros and cons, all the while aware that he was cursed. No matter what he did, he always chose the wrong option. To help him, Delphine advised: "You always get it wrong. So if you want a crêpe *complète*, choose a *forestière* instead."

5 Who was also, in fact, the owner: as with the Picks, it was a couple who owned and ran the restaurant.

"Good idea."

The owner listened to this dialogue without saying anything, but when she passed on the order to her husband, she added: "Just to warn you, they're psychopaths." A little later, while enjoying his crêpe, Frédéric admitted that his girlfriend had solved his problem: all he had to do was go against his instincts.

6

As they ate lunch, they dwelt on the story of the manuscript they had discovered.

"This is our Vivian Maier," said Delphine.

"Who?"

"You know, that wonderful photographer whose pictures weren't found until after her death."

"Oh yeah, you're right. Pick is our Vivian…"

"It's practically the same story. And people adore stuff like that."

THE STORY OF VIVIAN MAIER
(1926–2009)

In Chicago, a somewhat eccentric American woman of French origin had spent her life taking photographs without ever showing them to anybody, without ever thinking of exhibiting them, and often without even having enough money to have the pictures developed. Consequently, she never even got to see a large part of her work, but she was aware that she had talent. So why did she never try to make a living from her art? Instead, wearing baggy dresses and an old-fashioned hat, she earned money as a nanny. The children she looked after could never forget her, and particularly not the camera that she always wore on a strap around her neck. But who could have guessed just how good she was?

This woman, who ended up destitute, living on the margins of society, left behind thousands of photographs whose value has gone up every day since their discovery. At the end of her life, while she was hospitalized and incapable of paying rent on the lock-up garage where she kept the fruit of her artistic life, the boxes containing her photographs were auctioned off. A young man who was preparing to make a film about Chicago in the 1960s bought them all for a paltry sum. He typed the photographer's name into Google, but nothing appeared. When he created a website to display the work of this unknown photographer, he received hundreds of comments raving about it. Vivian Maier's pictures could not leave anyone indifferent. A few months later, he typed her name into a search engine again, and this time found her obituary. Two brothers had organized the funeral for their former nanny. The young man called them, and that was how he discovered that the genius whose photographs he owned had worked most of her life as a childminder.

It's the perfect example of somebody living an artistic life in almost total secrecy. Viviane Maier was not interested in fame, or in showing people her work. Nowadays, her photographs are exhibited all over the world and she is considered one of the great artists of the twentieth century. She had a unique way of capturing scenes of everyday life from unusual angles. But it's undeniable that a large part of her current fame derives from the way in which she was discovered, by chance, after her death.

64

*

For Delphine, the comparison with Pick was justified. This was a Breton pizzeria owner who, in absolute secrecy, had written a great novel. A man who had never tried to be published. Of course it would intrigue people. She started bombarding her boyfriend with questions: "When do you think he would have done his writing? What was his state of mind? Why did he never show anybody his book?" Frédéric tried to respond, like a novelist attempting to define the psychology of one of his characters.

7

Pick would come to the restaurant very early each morning, Madeleine had said. Perhaps he wrote then, while the pizza dough was resting? And then he hid his typewriter when his wife arrived. That way, nobody would know. Everybody has a sort of secret garden. His was writing. It would only be logical that he didn't try to publish his novel, Frédéric continued. He had no desire to share his inner passion with anyone. Hearing about the library of rejected books, he decided to deposit his manuscript there. But one detail in this story struck Delphine as odd: why put his name on the book? At any moment, someone could have seen that and made the connection. There was a discrepancy between this subterranean life and the risk of being caught like that. Presumably he guessed that nobody would bother rummaging around those shelves at the back of the library, said Frédéric. It was like a message in a bottle. Write a book, and leave it somewhere. And who knows? Perhaps one day it will be discovered.

Delphine thought of another detail. Magali had explained that the authors had to come to the library in person to leave their manuscripts. It was hard to believe that such a secretive man would have agreed to this demand. He probably knew Gourvec, since they'd lived in the same neighbourhood for half a century. What was the nature of their relationship? Perhaps librarians take an oath, like doctors, suggested Frédéric. Perhaps they are sworn to professional secrecy. Or perhaps Pick had told Gourvec when he dropped off his book: "Jean-Pierre, I'm relying on you not to breathe a word of this when you come to eat pizza at my restaurant…" A sentence that seems a little weak for a secret literary genius, but perhaps that's what happened.

Delphine and Frédéric took great pleasure in putting together all these theories, in trying to flesh out the novel behind the novel. Then the author of *The Bathtub* had a brilliant idea: "What if I wrote this story? A behind-the-scenes account of our discovery."

"Yes, that's a very good idea."

"I could call it *The Manuscript Found in Crozon*."

"Nice reference."

"Or maybe *The Library of Rejected Books*. Do you like that?"

"Yes, that's even better," Delphine replied. "To be honest, as long as you're publishing your books with me, and not with Gallimard, I'm happy with any title you come up with."

8

That evening at the Desperos' house, the famous novel was all anybody talked about. Fabienne thought it highly personal: "It seems to be autobiographical, and it's set in Brittany…" Delphine had not even considered this aspect of the novel. She was hoping that Madeleine wouldn't see it that way, because if she did she might be opposed to its publication. There would be time, later, to rummage through Pick's life and discover whether or not there really was a personal resonance to the book. In the end, the young editor decided to take her mother's comments as an encouraging sign: when you like a book, you want to know more about it. How much of it is true? What did the author actually experience? Much more so than for the other arts, which are figurative, there is a constant hunt for the personal in literature. Unlike Gustave Flaubert with his Emma, Leonardo da Vinci could never say: "The Mona Lisa is me."

Of course it was pointless to speculate, but Delphine could already imagine readers unpicking Pick's life. Anything could happen with this book, she could sense it. Although it has to be said that nothing is predictable. How many editors sure of having a bestseller on their hands have ended up with a flop? Then again, how many huge successes have come out of nowhere? For now, she needed to concentrate on convincing Pick's widow to let her publish the book.

She was nervous about the possibility that Madame Pick would refuse to sign the contract. Frédéric sought to reassure her: "Why would she refuse? Surely it's a nice surprise to find out you've spent your life with the Fitzgerald of pizza without realizing it…"

"Probably. But she would also be discovering that she spent her life with a stranger."

Delphine was apprehensive about the shock that this revelation might produce. Madeleine had clearly said that her husband never read books. But perhaps Frédéric was right: the news they were about to give her was positive, gratifying. After all, it wasn't the existence of another woman they were going to reveal, but a novel.[6]

9

Late that morning, Delphine and Frédéric rang the doorbell at Madame Pick's house. She quickly opened the door and invited them in. To avoid getting to the point too directly, they talked for a while about the weather, and then about Madeleine's friend whom she had visited in the hospital. Frédéric, who had asked about her, was so bad at appearing interested in the subject that she replied: "Do you really want to know?"

"…"

"I'll go make some tea."

Madeleine headed for the kitchen, giving Delphine an opportunity to glare at her boyfriend. Sometimes the person

6 Some would say that it amounts to the same thing.

you love can turn into a caricature in your eyes; for Delphine, Frédéric had become the typical social misfit, while he saw in her a portrait of overweening ambition. She lectured him in a harsh whisper: "Don't start trying to suck up to her. She likes honesty. That's obvious, don't you think?"

"I was just trying to create a climate of trust. And don't get all sanctimonious on me. I bet you've already printed out the contract, haven't you?"

"No!"

"But you've written it on your computer, right?"

"Maybe."

"I knew it! What kind of royalties are you offering her?"

"Ten per cent," she admitted, blushing slightly.

"And film and TV rights?"

"Fifty–fifty. The standard split. You think it could be a film?"

"Oh yes, definitely. Maybe even an American remake. It could take place in San Francisco. I can see the mist-veiled landscapes now…"

"Here's your caramel tea," announced Madeleine, suddenly appearing in the living room and interrupting the whispered conversation. Could she ever have imagined that her guests were already thinking of casting George Clooney in the role of her husband?

Frédéric, just as obsessed by the clock as he had been the day before, wondered how anybody could think clearly in a room filled by such a tyrannical ticking. He tried to think during the silences between the seconds, but it was as impossible as trying to walk between raindrops. But mostly what he thought was that he should just let Delphine do the talking; she was so much better at it.

"Have you been to the Crozon library?" she began.

"Of course, yes. I knew Gourvec, the old librarian. He was a nice man, very passionate about his books. But why are you asking me? Do you want me to borrow a book?"

"No, not at all. I mentioned it because there's something unusual about that library. Maybe you already know about it?"

"No, I have no idea. Listen, why don't you stop beating about the bush and just tell me what you want? I don't have that much time left, you know!" she replied in the same sarcastic voice that unsettled her guests and prevented them from relaxing into a smile.

So Delphine started talking about the library in a roundabout way. Why has this young woman come to my house to go on about the local library? Madeleine wondered. She wasn't surprised that Gourvec would have come up with that idea about the rejected books. She'd said nice things about him, out of politeness and respect for the dead, but in her opinion he had always been a bit mad. Some people had thought him cultured, but Madeleine had always considered him an eternal adolescent incapable of adapting to adult life. Every time she saw him, she always thought of a derailed train. Besides, she knew things. She had known his wife, for a start. The whole town had argued over the reasons for her disappearance, but Madeleine knew the truth. She knew exactly why Gourvec's wife had fled.

When you want something, you have to prolong the conversation, thought Delphine. So she laid on the details, some of them completely made up, as she retold the story of the library. Frédéric watched her, fascinated, wondering if she was the one who ought to be a novelist. She was quite masterly in her evocation of an era that she had barely known at all. You could sense the sincerity of her desire pulsing beneath her words. Finally, Delphine got to the heart of the matter, asking questions about Henri. The widow talked about him as if he still existed. Looking at Frédéric, she said: "That armchair you're sitting in was his. Nobody else was allowed to use it. When he came home late at night, he liked to sit there. It was his way of taking a break. I liked to watch him then, the dreamy look on his face. I could tell it did him good. Because, you know, he worked all the time. One day, I tried to calculate the number of pizzas he'd made. I think it was in the tens of thousands. That's quite a lot, when you think about it. So, yes, he was fond of that armchair..." Frédéric wanted to sit somewhere else, but Madeleine held him in place. "There's no point. He's not coming back."

Madeleine's hard, ironic facade melted now, to reveal a face that was much more human and emotional. The same transformation had occurred the day before: at the mention of her husband, her cynicism gave way to her truth, the pain of being a widow. Delphine hesitated: perhaps this revelation would upset her too much? She shared her concern in a brief exchange of glances with Frédéric, and for a moment she was tempted to forget the whole thing.

"But why are you asking me all these questions about the past?" Madeleine said.

Her question went unanswered. An awkward silence settled in the room, and even the ticking of the clock seemed less loud in Frédéric's ears. Or was he just getting used to it?

At last Delphine replied: "In that library of rejected books, we found a novel written by your husband."

"By my husband? You're joking!"

"The manuscript is signed Henri Pick, and as far as we know there is nobody else with that name. And it mentioned that he lived in Crozon, so it can only be him."

"You think my Henri wrote a book? Frankly, I'd be amazed. He never wrote me a single word. Not even a poem. It's not possible. I just can't imagine him writing anything!"

"And yet he did. Maybe in the restaurant, every morning, he would write for an hour or two…"

"And he never gave me flowers!"

"I don't see the connection," said Delphine, puzzled.

Madeleine shrugged. "I don't know… I'm just saying…"

Frédéric thought this invisible connection between writing and flowers was very beautiful. It was a daring imaginative leap in Madeleine's mind, as if those nonexistent petals were the visual transposition of an aptitude for writing.

10

The old woman continued the conversation, although it was clear she didn't really believe what they were saying. Perhaps someone else had written her husband's name on the manuscript, had hidden behind his identity?

"That's not possible. Gourvec only accepted manuscripts that were handed over in person. And the date on the manuscript is from the very start of the library's creation."

"You expect me to trust Gourvec? Who says that *he* didn't use my husband's name?"

Delphine didn't know how to reply to this. After all, what Madeleine said was possible. For now, apart from his name on the manuscript, there was nothing to prove that this novel had indeed been written by Henri Pick.

"You told us that your husband loved Russia," Frédéric reminded her.

"Yeah. So?"

"His novel is partly about the great Russian poet, Pushkin."

"Who?"

"Alexander Pushkin. He's not that famous in France. You'd really have to be a fan of Russian culture to write about him…"

"Let's not get carried away. Just because he named a pizza after Stalin doesn't mean he read Pushkin. I think you're both a bit odd, I have to say."

"The best thing would be for you to read the novel," Delphine interjected. "I'm sure you will recognize your husband's voice. You know, it's really quite common for people to have a secret passion, something they don't want to share. Maybe you have one too?"

"No. I like embroidery. But why would I hide that from Henri?"

73

"No secrets?" asked Frédéric. "I'm sure you must have kept some things hidden from your husband. Everybody has secrets, don't they?"

Madeleine did not like the way this conversation was going. Who did these people think they were? And this whole thing about the novel, she just couldn't believe it. Henri, a writer? He hadn't even written the day's specials on the chalkboard outside the restaurant; she'd been the one to do that. So how could he have theorized about some Russian poet? And a love story! That was what the two young people had said. A love story? Henri? He'd never even written her a Valentine's Day card. So the idea that he had a whole novel in his head... come on, it just wasn't possible. The only notes he'd ever left for her were invariably about the logistics of running the pizzeria. "Don't forget to buy flour; call the carpenter about the new chairs; order Chianti." And that man was supposed to have written a novel? She didn't believe it... although she knew from experience that people were capable of surprising you. Many times, she'd heard stories about people living double lives.

She started thinking about all the things Henri hadn't known about her. Her private, inaccessible self. All the things she'd hidden from him, her economies with the truth. He knew her likes and dislikes, her past and her family, but all the rest was a mystery to him. He didn't know anything about her nightmares or her desires; he knew nothing about the lover she'd had in 1972 and the pain of never having seen him since then; he didn't know that she had actually wanted another child, despite what she'd told him, and that the truth was simply that she couldn't get pregnant again. The more she thought about it, the more she had to admit that her husband knew her in only an incomplete way. Which meant that this thing about the novel could be true. She had caricatured Henri; it was true that he didn't read and didn't seem interested in literature, but she'd always thought he had a unique way of looking at life. She used to say that he had a noble mind; he never judged people, always took his time before advancing an opinion on anyone. He was a man with a good sense of proportion, at ease with the idea that he had to detach himself from the world in order to understand it. By refining his portrait in this way, she made it less impossible to imagine her husband as a writer.

A few minutes later, she even thought it was possible. Improbable, sure, but possible. And there was something else to bear in mind: she liked this manifestation of the past. She wanted to believe anything that enabled her to be in contact with Henri again, the way some people start playing with Ouija boards. Perhaps he left this novel for her? So he could surprise her by returning. So he could tell her that he was still there; perhaps this novel was a way of whispering his presence into her ear, so that their past could live again. So she asked: "Can I read his book?"

I I

On the way back to Morgat, Frédéric tried to console his disappointed girlfriend. Perhaps it was for the best that they hadn't immediately discussed publication. By taking things slowly, they would give the widow time to come to terms with the revelation. Once she'd read the novel, she would have no more doubts. A book like that could not be left in the shadows for much longer. Surely she would feel immensely proud to have been the companion of the man who had written such a novel; she could always tell people that she was his inspiration. You don't have to be young and beautiful to be a muse.

I 2

Readers always find themselves in a book, in one way or another. Reading is a completely egotistical pleasure. Unconsciously we expect books to speak to us. An author can write the most far-fetched or implausible story ever, but there will still be readers who will say: "I don't believe it: you wrote the story of my life!"

Where Madeleine was concerned, this feeling was understandable. It was perhaps her husband who had written this novel. So, more than anyone, she sought out resonances with their life together. She was disconcerted by the way he described the coast of Brittany; it seemed very perfunctory for a man who had this region in his blood. But she supposed it was a way of saying that the background wasn't important. What mattered was intimacy, the precision of emotions. And there was so much of that. She was surprised by the sensual, even erotic, descriptions. In Madeleine's eyes, her husband had always seemed attentive but a bit boorish; kindly, but not really romantic. In the novel, there was such delicacy of feeling between the characters. And it was so sad. They embraced before abandoning each other forever. They touched each other with a desperate desire. The author represented the last hours of a love affair through the metaphor of a slowly dying candle, consuming itself in a frenzy of flickering light. You kept thinking that the flame had gone out, but it kept being resurrected and its survival was so beautiful; it went on for hours, a symbol of hope.

How could her husband have nurtured such an expression of intensity? In truth, reading the novel spirited Madeleine back to the beginning of their own love. It all came back to her now. She remembered how, in the summer of her seventeenth year, she had to leave with her parents for two months, to visit family in the north of France. She and Henri were already in love, and the thought of that separation was so painful. They spent a whole afternoon together, their bodies entwined, trying to memorize every detail of each other, the two of them promising that they would think about their love all the time. She had completely forgotten that episode, until now. And yet it was at the very root of their love; their hearts had grown fonder during that long, forced absence. When they saw each other again, in September, they had sworn never to be apart again.

Madeleine was deeply moved. Her husband had kept within him that fear of losing her, and he'd transcribed it into words years later. She didn't understand why he hadn't wanted to show her his writing, but undoubtedly he had his reasons. Anyway, it was certain now: Henri had written a book. Madeleine let go of her initial incredulity and gave herself entirely to this new reality.

13

When she had finished reading, Madeleine called Delphine. Her voice had changed; it was thick with emotion. She wanted to say that it was a beautiful novel, but she couldn't. Instead, she invited the young couple to visit her again the next day.

That night, she woke up and reread a few passages. It was as if, with this novel, Henri had returned from the dead to see her again, to tell her: "Don't forget me." And yet she *had* forgotten him. Not completely, of course; she thought about him quite often. But, deep down, she had got used to living alone. People had praised her strength and her courage, but it hadn't really been all that hard. She had prepared herself for the final deadline, and when it came she had accepted it almost peacefully. You can get used to what once seemed unbearable more easily than you expect. And now he had come back to her in the form of a novel.

When the young couple arrived, Madeleine tried to put her feelings into words: "It's just strange, Henri returning like that. It's like I didn't know him before."

"No, you shouldn't think of it like that," Delphine replied. "It was his secret. He probably didn't have much self-confidence."

"You think?"

"Yes. Or maybe he didn't tell you about it because he wanted to surprise you. But as nobody wanted to publish it, he left his novel in a drawer. And later, when Gourvec opened his library of rejects, he decided that was the perfect resting place."

"Maybe. Anyway, I'm no expert, but I thought it was beautiful. And the story about the poet was very interesting too."

"Yes, it's really a wonderful novel," Delphine repeated.

"I think it must have been inspired by our two-month separation when we were seventeen," added Madeleine.

"Oh really?" asked Frédéric.

"Yes. Well, he changed a lot of things."

"That's normal," said Delphine. "It's a novel. But if you found yourself in the story, then there's no doubt any more."

"No, probably not."

"You still have doubts?"

"I don't know. I feel a bit lost."

"I understand," said Delphine, putting her hand on Madeleine's.

After a while, the old woman spoke again: "My husband left lots of cardboard boxes in the attic. I can't go up there. But when he died, Joséphine took a look at them."

"Joséphine is your daughter?" asked Delphine.

"Yes."

"Did she find anything interesting?"

"No. She told me it was mostly old account books for the restaurant. But we should take another look. She didn't spend long up there. Maybe he left some explanation, or another book…"

"Yes, we should take a look," said Frédéric before heading towards the toilet. In fact, he wanted to leave Delphine alone with Madeleine because he sensed that she was about to talk about publication.

Frédéric wandered around the house, examining each bedroom. He saw a man's slippers, presumably Henri's.[7] He stared at them for a moment, and gradually they were replaced by a vision of Pick. He was like Bartleby, the Herman Melville hero. The scrivener who constantly declares that he would *prefer not to*, in his tenacious determination to avoid all action. That character had become a symbol of renunciation. Frédéric had always loved Bartleby, with his subtle social protest, and *The Bathtub* had been partly inspired by him. Pick, he thought, was a similar character. There was a sort of rejection of the world in his attitude, as if he were driven by an ambition for obscurity, a figure swimming against the tide of an era where everybody seeks the limelight.

7 Would a woman keep *his* slippers after he died? he wondered.

PART FOUR

I

IN THE CORRIDORS and offices of the publishing house, tongues began to wag: a major book was in the offing. Delphine had realized that the best way to publicize the novel was to talk about it as little as possible, to let a feeling of mystery surround it, perhaps even a few false rumours. When people asked her about the book, she replied simply: it's by a dead Breton author. Certain sentences have a unique ability to end a conversation.

2

Frédéric pretended to be jealous: "All you care about these days is Pick. What about my *Bed*? Aren't you interested in that any more?" Sometimes Delphine would reassure him with words, and sometimes with her body. She dressed the way he wanted, so that he would undress her the way she wanted. Their desire did not require artifice to remain intense, and physical love continued to be their most fluent form of conversation. Time had flown since their first meeting; minutes speeding by with little chance for drawing breath. Weariness seemed an impossibility.

In other moments, they had to express themselves in words. Frédéric's jealousy of Pick was a recurring theme. Delphine was annoyed by her boyfriend's childishness. Too much writing can turn you into a spoilt kid. Sometimes she wanted to shake him. Deep down, though, she liked his fears. She felt useful to this man; she perceived his fragilities not as insuperable flaws, but as superficial wounds. Frédéric was not really weak; his strength was just hidden behind his apparent aimlessness. In order to write, he needed two contradictory forms of energy. He felt lost and melancholic, but at heart he had a worldly ambition.

One other thing must be made clear: Frédéric hated meetings. Nothing wearied him more than the idea of seeing somebody in a café to have a discussion. He thought there was something incongruous about the way humans felt the need to meet up to chat about things for an hour or two. He preferred communing with the city—or walking, in other words. After writing in the morning, he would wander the streets, trying to observe everything, particularly women. Occasionally he would pass a bookshop, and it was always a bitter experience. He would enter that place designed to depress anyone who has published a book, and make himself feel terrible by searching for his novel. Of course, *The Bathtub* was nowhere to be found now. But perhaps one bookshop owner might have forgotten to return it to the publisher, or even decided to keep it on his shelves? In fact, he was simply searching for proof of its existence, wracked as he was by doubt. Had he really published a book? He needed the bite of reality to feel certain.

One day, he bumped into an ex-girlfriend, Agathe. He hadn't seen her in over five years. A lifetime ago. Their reunion plunged him back into a time when he was a different man. The Frédéric that Agathe had gone out with was a sort of unfinished version, a rough draft. She was more beautiful now, as if she had not been able to fully bloom in his presence. Their break-up had not been dramatic; they had come to a mutual agreement: a cold, legalistic expression that ultimately evokes the mutual agreement that there was no love between them. They got on fairly well, but they never saw each other again after their split. They had stopped calling, stopped texting. There was nothing left to say. They had loved each other and then they had stopped loving each other.

Eventually the question of what they were up to now arose. "What are you doing these days?" Agathe asked. Frédéric felt like saying "Nothing." But in the end he decided to mention the fact that he was writing his second novel. Her face lit up. "Oh really? You published a book?" She seemed happy that his dream had finally come true, but unwittingly her words pierced him to the core. If this woman whom he had loved, whom he had been with for nearly three years, the smell of whose armpits he remembered perfectly, didn't know that he had published *The Bathtub*, then his failure was unbearable. He pretended that he was happy to have seen her again, and left without asking her a single question. He hasn't changed, she thought: it's all about him. She had no idea that she had hurt him.

It was a new order of narcissistic wound; she was part of what we might call *the inner circle*. In some way, it was against the rules for Agathe not to know that he had published a novel. Frédéric himself was so stunned by the importance he gave to this information that he decided it was better to end the conversation. Then, suddenly, he got it into his head to go after her. Thankfully she moved very slowly; that hadn't changed. Agathe had always walked the way some people read books: without ever skipping a word. When he caught up with her, he watched her for a few seconds before pronouncing her name with his mouth close to her ear. She turned, wide-eyed: "Oh, it's you! You scared me."

"Yes, sorry. I was just thinking that our conversation was too brief. You didn't tell me anything about yourself. Would you like to go for a coffee?"

3

Madeleine was still struggling to accept the idea that her husband had never told her about his passion for literature. Her past had taken on another tone now, like a scene or a landscape viewed from the other side. It bothered her, and she wondered whether she should lie. She could easily say that yes, she knew Henri had written a book. Who could contradict her? But no, she couldn't do that. She had to respect his desire for silence. But why had he hidden everything? Those few pages had created a gulf between them. She knew perfectly well that he couldn't have written a book like that in a few weeks. It must represent months, even years, of work.

Every day, he had lived with that story inside his mind. And in the evenings, when they lay in bed together, he must still have been thinking about his novel. But whenever he talked to her, the only things he mentioned were problems with customers or suppliers.

Another question haunted her: would Henri have wanted his novel to be published? After all, he'd left it in that library instead of just getting rid of it. Presumably he had hoped that somebody would read it. But how could she be sure? What could she possibly know about his wishes? Everything was so confused. After a while, she decided that it would be a way of bringing him back to life. In the end, that was all that mattered. People would talk about him; he would be alive again. That is the privilege of artists: to outfox death by leaving behind their creations. And what if this were just the start? What if he had performed other acts in his life that would be discovered later? Perhaps he was one of those men who exist only in their absence.

Since his death, she had never wanted to go up to the attic. Henri had kept cardboard boxes there, full of things accumulated over the years. She wasn't sure what she would find there. Joséphine had been in a rush the last time she looked through them; they needed to search more thoroughly. Maybe she would find another novel? But it was difficult to get up there. It involved climbing a stepladder, which she couldn't manage. That must have suited him, she thought; he could have put whatever he wanted up there, knowing that she could never find it. She had to call her daughter. It would give her a chance to finally bring up the subject of her father's novel; Madeleine had found it impossible to talk to her daughter about this before. True, they didn't speak often, but she should really have mentioned it earlier. The truth was that the revelation about the novel had plunged Madeleine into a new relationship with her husband, a relationship into which she had found it hard to integrate the presence of their daughter. But she couldn't keep her out of it much longer. The book would be published soon. Joséphine would be bound to react like she had; she would be shocked, stupefied. Madeleine feared that moment for another, related reason: her daughter exhausted her.

4

Joséphine was in her early fifties, and since her divorce she had completely let herself go. She couldn't string two sentences together without breathing hard. A few years before, almost simultaneously, her two daughters and her husband had all left the family home: the two girls to live their lives, and the man to live without her. After giving everything, she felt, to build a fulfilling life for each of them, she had been left alone. The after-effects of this emotional shock fluctuated between melancholy and aggression. There was something distressing about seeing this woman, well known for her energy and her plain speaking, sink into depression. It might just have been a phase, a testing moment, but the pain grew roots; it grafted a new skin, sad and bitter, onto her body. Thankfully, she liked her job. She ran a lingerie shop, and spent her days there in a cocoon that protected her from the brutality beyond.

Her daughters had gone to Berlin together to open a restaurant, and Joséphine had visited them a few times. Walking around that city, simultaneously modern and scarred by its past, she came to understand that it was possible to move beyond devastation not by forgetting it but by accepting it. It was possible to build happiness on a foundation filled with suffering. But this was easier said than done, and human beings had less time to rebuild themselves than cities did. Joséphine often spoke with her daughters on the phone, but it wasn't the same; she wanted to see them. Her ex-husband called her occasionally too, to ask how she was, but it felt like a chore, like a sort of post-break-up aftersales service. When she talked to him, he always played down the happiness of his new life, but she could tell he was deeply content. Of course, he didn't like to think of the damage he had left behind him, but there comes an age when time is ticking and it becomes impossible to renounce pleasure.

Eventually, the spaces between their phone calls grew longer and longer, and it was now several months since Joséphine had heard from Marc. She couldn't even bear to pronounce his name. She didn't want it in her mouth: this was her tiny victory over her own body. But he was on her mind all the time. He was also in Rennes, the city where they had lived together, and where he lived now with his new lover. The one who leaves should at least have the decency to move away, she thought. Joséphine considered her city as an accomplice in this emotional tragedy. Geography always takes the victors' side. Joséphine lived in fear of bumping into her ex-husband, of accidentally witnessing his happiness, so she never left her neighbourhood now, *the capital of her pain.*

This was not the only loss she had suffered: her father had died too. It was difficult to claim they had been close, because he had been stingy with his affections. But he had always been a protective presence in her life. As a child, she'd spent hours in the restaurant, watching him make pizzas. He'd even named one of them after her: a chocolate pizza, the Pizza Joséphine. She was fascinated by this father of hers, braving the heat of that immense oven. And Henri liked to feel his daughter's admiring gaze. It's so easy to be a hero in the eyes of a child. Joséphine often thought about that lost time; never again would she be able to enter a pizzeria. She liked the idea that her daughters were carrying the torch of their grandfather's vocation, making Breton crêpes for the Germans. This was how a family threaded its way through history. But what remained of that thread now? The shock of her divorce had aggravated her grief over her father. Perhaps, if she could just rest her head against his shoulder, everything would be all right again, as it had been before. His body as a shield against the world. His body, which sometimes appeared to her in dreams, so vivid, so real; but he never spoke during his nocturnal visits. He passed through her dreams as he had passed through her life, in reassuring silence.

Joséphine had liked one thing in particular about her father: he never wasted his time criticizing people. Presumably he still had those thoughts, but he didn't squander his energy uselessly. Some people thought him introverted, but his daughter had always considered him a sort of wise man, out of sync with the world. And now he wasn't there any more. He was rotting in the Crozon cemetery. She was rotting too. She was alive, but her reason for living had been buried. Marc didn't want her any more. Madeleine, although saddened by her daughter's divorce, could not understand why Joséphine didn't just move on. Born to a poor family, and having lived through the war, Madeleine considered crying over love to be a privilege of the modern world. Joséphine should *start a new life* instead of whining and snivelling. Joséphine, for her part, was exasperated by this idea. What had she ever done wrong? Why should she have to start a new life when she'd been perfectly happy with the old one?

Recently, she had begun going to church; she found some comfort in religion. To be honest, though, it wasn't faith that drew her, but the place itself. It was a timeless space, safe from the brutality of life's perils. She believed less in God than in His house. Her daughters worried about this transformation, considering it out of character for a woman who had always been so pragmatic. From Berlin, they encouraged her to go out, have a social life, but she had no desire for anything like that. Why did your loved ones always want you to get over things? What if she didn't want her wounds to heal?

All the same, to appease her friends, she had gone out on a few dates. Each time, it had been a miserable experience. There had been one man who, after driving her home, had put his hand between her thighs, clumsily searching for her clitoris before he had even kissed her. Surprised by this abrupt (to say the least) attack, she had roughly pushed him away. Not discouraged in the least, he had whispered a few rude, even quite disgusting phrases into her ear, thinking they would excite her. Joséphine had got out of the car, laughing hysterically. Obviously it had not been what she was looking for, but it was a relief all the same: she hadn't laughed like that in years. The man probably felt embarrassed now at having rushed things; she imagined he regretted offering to handcuff her on their first date, but he'd read somewhere that women adored that sort of thing.

5

On the way, Joséphine thought about her mother's words: "You have to come and see me, it's urgent." She had not wanted to say anything more than that on the phone, although she had made clear that nothing terrible had happened. It was an unusual situation; completely unprecedented, in fact. Madeleine never asked her daughter for anything. In reality, they barely spoke to each other. They were so different that silence was the best way of avoiding arguments. While Madeleine was bored with her daughter's complaints, Joséphine was simply desperate for a hint of tenderness, a motherly hug. But she knew she shouldn't necessarily see her mother's apparent coldness as a form of rejection. It was a generational thing. Her parents' generation didn't love each other less, they just showed it less.

When Joséphine returned to Crozon, she slept in her childhood bedroom. Each time, the memories came back to her; she saw herself again as a mischievous little girl, as a grumpy teenager, as a provocative young woman. All the Joséphines were there, as in a retrospective exhibition. Nothing changed here. Even her mother seemed to her to be the same eternally ageless woman. It was still the case today.

Joséphine kissed her mother and immediately asked her what was so urgent. But Madeleine preferred to take her time; she made some tea and calmly sat down before saying: "I've discovered something about your father."

"What? Don't tell me he had another child."

"No, of course not!"

"Oh. What, then?"

"He wrote a novel."

"Papa? A novel? Don't be ridiculous."

"But it's true. I read it."

"He never wrote anything. He never even signed birthday cards—it was always your handwriting. Postcards, letters... nothing. And you expect me to believe that he wrote a novel?"

"I'm telling you, it's the truth."

"Oh yeah, I know how this works. You think I'm completely depressed, so you tell me some rubbish to make me react. I read an article about it—'mythotherapy' or something, right?"

"..."

"I don't get why it bothers you so much that I see the world as a dark place. It's my life, I'll live it how I want. You're always so cheerful. People love you, with your larger-than-life personality! Well, I'm sorry, but I'm not like you. I'm weak, anxious, gloomy."

In reply to this, Madeleine stood up to fetch the manuscript, which she handed to her daughter. "Calm down, will you? This is the book."

"But... what is it? Recipes?"

"No. I told you, it's a novel. A love story."

"A love story?"

"And it's going to be published."

"What?"

"Yes. I'll tell you all the details later."

"..."

"I wanted you to come so you could go up to the attic. I know you've already been up there, but not for long. Maybe if you have a better look, you'll find some other things."

Joséphine did not respond. She was hypnotized by the manuscript's first page, with her father's name at the top: Henri Pick. And then the title:

The Last Hours of a Love Affair

6

For a long moment, Joséphine was speechless, hovering between incredulity and stupefaction. Madeleine realized that the exploration of the attic would have to wait. Particularly since her daughter had already started reading the novel. Joséphine rarely read books at all. She preferred women's magazines or celebrity gossip. The last book she'd read was *Thank You for This Moment* by Valérie Trierweiler, the former partner of the French president François Hollande; the book was a memoir about their relationship and break-up. For obvious reasons, the subject had been close to Joséphine's heart. She'd identified completely with the scorned woman. If she could have, she'd have written a book about Marc. But nobody was interested in that idiot. Of course, she thought that Trierweiler had gone too far, but this woman no longer cared what anyone thought of her. Expressing her pain, and taking revenge, had become more important than her own image. She was a suicide bomber of love, preferring to blow up everything along with her past. Joséphine understood this. She, too, put herself in danger sometimes, in her relationships with other women, or by exhausting her friends and family with her endless litany of disappointments. So many feelings swirled inside her that her mind grew confused. The hated man became a dark beast in a distorted reality, a monster as vast as the wounded woman's suffering; a man who no longer exists the way he is described or imagined.

Joséphine kept reading without difficulty. She didn't recognize her father's voice, but then she hadn't imagined he was even capable of writing a book. Yet what she felt echoed a sensation that she had never been able to define. She had often had the feeling of not being able to tell what he was thinking. To her, he seemed unfathomable, and that quality had grown in his later years, after he retired. He would spend hours staring at the sea, as if halted within himself. In the evening, he would go out to drink beer with the regulars at the local café, but he never seemed to get drunk. And whenever he saw someone he knew in the street, Joséphine noticed that they never said much to each other—just a few indistinct words—and she felt sure that his evenings in the café were above all an attempt to stave off boredom. Now she thought that all his silences, the way he gradually erased himself from the world, had perhaps been a way of hiding his poetic soul.

Joséphine said that the story reminded her of the Clint Eastwood film, *The Bridges of Madison County*.

"Clint who? The bridges of what?" her mother demanded.

"Never mind…"

"So shall we go up to the attic?"

"Okay."

"Get up, then."

"I just can't get my head around this whole thing."

"Me neither."

"You never know anyone. Especially not a man," said Joséphine, incapable of going more than two minutes without relating everything back to her own life.

Finally she went to get the small stepladder necessary to reach the attic. She opened the trapdoor and climbed, bent double, into that dusty nook. Her gaze was immediately drawn to a small wooden rocking horse that she used to ride as a child. Then she saw a blackboard. She'd forgotten that her parents never threw anything away. She found her dolls, all of which had the strange particularity of not wearing clothes, only knickers. It was crazy to think that she was already obsessed with underwear at that age. A little further on, she glimpsed a pile of her father's aprons. A whole career encapsulated in a few scraps of fabric. At last, she saw the cardboard boxes that her mother had mentioned. She opened the first one, and it took her only a few seconds to make a crucial discovery.

PART FIVE

I

DELPHINE EXPLAINED the project to Grasset's sales representatives. These men and women would travel all over France, announcing to booksellers that a very unusual book was about to be published. For the young editor, this first public presentation was an important test. They had not yet read the novel; how would they react to the story of its discovery? She'd asked Olivier Nora, her boss, to give her more time than usual so she could go through all the details. From the beginning, the novel of the novel would be crucially important. Of course Olivier had agreed; he, too, was unusually excited by the project. Several times, he'd repeated disbelievingly: "You were on holiday at your parents' place and you discovered a library of rejected books? It's incredible…" Normally a very elegant man with an almost British self-control, he had jubilantly rubbed his hands together like a child who'd just won at marbles.

The pleasure of presenting Pick's novel made Delphine even more radiant. In her high heels, she towered over the meeting room, although not in an oppressive way. She spoke with gentle assurance. She seemed certain that she had discovered a major author in the person of this dead pizzeria owner. The sales reps all appeared enthusiastic about the idea of championing this publication. They immediately started talking about window displays, which was very rare for a first novel. "The whole company believes in this," announced Olivier Nora. One of the reps mentioned that he remembered the library in Brittany; he'd read an article about it a long time ago. Sabine Richer, head of the Touraine region and a big fan of American literature, talked about the Richard Brautigan novel that had been at the origin of the idea. She adored that novel—an epic road trip to Mexico, in which the author cast an ironic glance over 1960s California. Jean-Paul Enthoven, a writer and editor, went into raptures about Sabine's erudition, and she blushed.

Delphine had never been to a presentation anything like this one. Usually, they were long, dull affairs, with everybody fastidiously taking notes about the upcoming releases. This time, something happened. They bombarded her with questions. One man, squeezed into a too-small suit, asked: "What about promoting the book? How will you do that?"

"There's his widow. An old Breton woman, eighty years old, good sense of humour. She knew nothing about her husband's secret life, and I can tell you it's pretty powerful when she talks about it."

"Did he write any other books?" the man asked.

"We don't think so. His wife and his daughter have searched the attic, and they didn't find another manuscript."

"But they did make an important discovery," said Olivier Nora. "Right, Delphine?"

"Yes. They found a book by Pushkin: *Yevgeny Onegin*."

"Why's that important?" another rep asked.

"Because Pushkin is at the very heart of the novel. And in the book that his wife discovered, Pick had underlined certain sentences. I'll have to get hold of that copy. He may have left some clues, or he may have wanted to communicate something by marking those passages."

"I have the feeling that there are more surprises to come," concluded Olivier Nora, as if to highlight the book's mysteriousness.

"*Yevgeny Onegin* is a wonderful novel in verse," interjected Jean-Paul Enthoven. "A few years ago, a Russian woman gave me a copy. A beautiful and very cultured woman. She tried to explain to me the beauty of Pushkin's language. No translation can convey that."

"And did he speak Russian, this Pick?" asked another rep.

"Not to my knowledge, but he adored Russia. He even named a pizza after Stalin," added Delphine.

"Is that how you want us to sell the novel to booksellers?" the man asked, chuckling, and the whole room roared with laughter.

The meeting went on like that for a while longer, with everybody talking about Pick's novel so much that there was little time left for the other books that would come out at the same time. This is often how the fate of a book is decided; some are given a head start. The publisher's enthusiasm is the deciding factor; every parent has a favourite child. *The Last Hours of a Love Affair* would be Grasset's lead title for the spring, and everybody at the company was hopeful that its success would last until the summer and beyond. Olivier Nora didn't want to wait until September so he could publish it in the famous French *rentrée littéraire*, which would have given the novel a better chance of competing for the big literary prizes. That period of the year was too competitive and overcrowded, and it was likely that nobody would see it as a true story, but rather as an attempt by a famous author to trick the critics and literary judges by hiding behind the facade of a dead pizzeria owner. It was, said Nora, simply an incredible story, unearthing a novel in this way. And it was important to believe, sometimes, in incredible stories.

2

Hervé Maroutou waited for a brief silence to bring up what he considered to be an important point. For years, he had been roaming the east of France three days a week, and he had established friendly relations with many booksellers. He knew each one's tastes, and that enabled him to personalize his catalogue presentations. A sales representative is an essential link in the bookselling chain, the human link to reality—and often that reality is one of suffering. Year after year, as book-shops closed, his rounds grew shorter; he was literally running out of road.

Maroutou was in awe of these foot soldiers of literature, who formed a bulwark against the coming world: a world that was not necessarily better or worse, but in which the book was no longer considered an essential aspect of culture. Hervé often met his competitors, and had become particularly friendly with Bernard Jean, his counterpart at Hachette. They would stay in the same hotels, eat the same all-inclusive "special representatives' menu" offered by certain Ibis establishments. Over dessert one evening, Hervé mentioned Pick's novel. Bernard Jean replied: "Isn't that a bit weird, publishing a rejected author?" This reaction, made at the exact moment when one of the men was eating a *tarte normande* and the other a chocolate mousse, had been anticipated by Maroutou during the meeting at Grasset. He was always one step ahead.

At the time, he'd asked Delphine: "Isn't it a risk, publishing a book by explaining that you found it in a library devoted to rejected manuscripts?"

"Of course not," the editor replied. "There's a long and venerable history of masterpieces rejected by publishers. I'll draw up a list, and that can be our response."

"That's very true," someone sighed.

"Besides, there's nothing to prove that Pick ever sent his manuscript to a publisher. In fact, I'm pretty sure that he took it straight to the library of rejects."

This last sentence changed the whole equation. Perhaps it was not a book that had been rejected, but one never intended for publication. It would be almost impossible to verify either way: publishers don't keep records of the books they've rejected. Delphine made preparations to respond confidently and vigorously to all such questions. She did not want anybody to doubt this book. She spoke about the beauty of not seeking publication, of living a life beyond the margins of worldly recognition. "He was a genius who loved obscurity, that's what we should say," she added. In an age where everybody wants to be famous for everything and nothing, here was a man who spent months of his life perfecting a work destined to be dust.

3

After that meeting, Delphine decide to prepare a few documents supporting the idea that rejection is no measure of a work's quality. *Swann's Way* by Marcel Proust is surely one of the most celebrated rejected books. There have been so many articles analysing the manuscript's failure with publishers that you could stitch them together into a book longer than the original novel. In 1912, Proust was known principally for his love of high society. Is that why he wasn't taken seriously? Mysterious recluses are always more appealing. The qualities of the silent and the sickly are more vaunted. But is it impossible to be at once brilliant and frivolous? A brief glance at the first volume of *In Search of Lost Time* was surely enough for anyone to recognize its literary quality. Gallimard's reading committee at the time was composed of famous writers, including André Gide. Perhaps he merely leafed through the book rather than reading it and, armed with his prejudices, found some sentences that he considered clumsy[8] and others that were tortuously long. Not taken seriously, roundly rejected, Proust was forced to pay for the book's publication himself. Gide would later admit that the rejection of that novel remained "the reading committee's greatest error". Gallimard responded by finally publishing Proust. In 1919, the second book in the series, *In the Shadow of Young Girls in Flower*, won the Prix Goncourt, and for the past century this author, initially turned down by every major publisher in France, has been considered one of the greatest writers of all time.

Another emblematic example is John Kennedy Toole's *A Confederacy of Dunces*. The author, exhausted by the constant rejection of his novel, committed suicide in 1969 at the age of thirty-one. With prophetic irony, the epigraph of his novel was a quote from Jonathan Swift: "When a true genius appears in the world, you may know him by this sign, that the dunces are all in confederacy against him." How is it possible that such a powerfully original and funny novel could not have found a publisher? After the author's death, his mother spent years devoting herself to getting the manuscript published. Her determination was rewarded, and when the book came out in 1980 it was a huge international success. It has become a classic of American literature. The story of the author, driven to suicide by the world's incomprehension of his brilliance, surely contributed to his posthumous fame. Many masterpieces are accompanied by a novel of the novel.

8   Such as the striking description of a character's forehead 'where the bones showed through like the points of a crown of thorns or the beads of a rosary'.

So Delphine noted down these examples, in case some critics mentioned the possibility that Pick's novel had been rejected. She also did some more research on Richard Brautigan. She had often heard authors refer to him—Philippe Jaenada,[9] for example—but she hadn't yet read any of his books. Sometimes you create an image in your head of an author just because of one title. Thanks to *Dreaming of Babylon*—translated into French as "A Private Detective in Babylon"—Delphine associated Brautigan with a hippie version of Philip Marlowe: a mix of Bogart and Kerouac. But reading Brautigan, she discovered his fragility, his humour, his irony, his subtle melancholy. She decided he was more like another American author that she'd just discovered, Steve Tesich, and his novel *Karoo*. To return to our theme of rejected books, Brautigan too had a hard time with rejections from publishers. Before becoming one of the most iconic authors of his generation, mobbed by groups of hippies, he had spent several years living close to the poverty line. Unable to pay his bus fare, he would sometimes walk three hours to an appointment; having hardly anything to eat, he didn't refuse when a friend offered him a sandwich. All those hard years had been punctuated by the regular thud of rejection slips landing from publishers. Nobody believed in him. Manuscripts that later became so successful were given no more than a quick, scornful glance. His idea for the library of rejected books was undoubtedly born during this period

9   An author she liked as much for his writing style as his physical appearance (like a mischievous bear), but whom she no longer saw very often, since he had left Grasset to return to his first publisher, Julliard.

when his words were ignored. He knew all too well what it
was to be a misunderstood artist.[10]

4

As the publication date drew nearer, despite the enthusiastic
responses of booksellers and critics, Delphine became increasingly stressed. It was the first time she had felt this kind of
anxiety about a book. She was always invested in her projects,
but Pick's book had driven her into a completely new state of
feverishness; the feeling of being on the edge of something
major.

Every evening, she called Madeleine to check how she was.
She thought it important to be there for her authors, and even
more so for the writer's widow. Perhaps she had a premonition
of what was going to happen? She had to prepare this elderly
woman for the limelight. Delphine was worried that Madeleine's
life would be turned upside down; she had not expected that.
Sometimes she felt uneasy at having convinced Madeleine to
publish her husband's book. This was not the editor's usual
role; this whole story could be perceived as a sort of hijacking
of fate, and perhaps as a lack of respect for an author's wishes.

Frédéric, meanwhile, was struggling to write his novel. In
these periods of literary difficulties, he had trouble with words

10   As if recognition consisted of *being understood*. Nobody is ever understood,
and certainly not writers. They wander through kingdoms of strange
emotions and, most of the time, do not even understand themselves.

in general: he never knew what to say to reassure Delphine. This lack of inspiration infected both of them, leaving their relationship like a blank page. The adventure, which had begun in Crozon with feelings of excitement and even joy, had become an oppressive, nerve-wracking exercise. They made love less often, and argued more. Frédéric felt bad, staying in the apartment all day long, going round in circles, waiting for his girlfriend to return as if she were the only proof of the existence of other humans. For a while now, he'd felt a need for attention, like a misbehaving child. So, one day, he announced coldly:

"I meant to say, I saw my ex again."

"Oh?"

"Yes, I bumped into her in the street. We went for coffee together."

Delphine didn't know what to say to this. Not that she was jealous, but Frédéric's vindictive tone had taken her by surprise. The brutal way he stated the facts suggested that the information was important. What had happened? In reality, the answer was: nothing. When he caught up with his ex on the street and suggested going out for a coffee, she said she couldn't. He had considered this a second humiliation. Which was ridiculous: she had been perfectly pleasant to him. Frédéric distorted reality, interpreting two harmless facts as marks of contempt. Agathe might have a meeting, and it wasn't her fault if her ex-boyfriend's novel had been published to so little fanfare that she'd never heard of it. Frédéric refused to see things this way; he was, perhaps, a little bit paranoid.

"Okay. So was it nice?" Delphine asked.

"Yes. We talked for two hours. The time just flew by!"

"Why are you saying it like that?"

"I'm just letting you know, that's all."

"Okay, but I'm really stressed at the moment. And for a good reason, as you know. So you could be a bit gentler with me."

"Calm down, nothing happened. I just had coffee with her, we didn't sleep together."

"All right. Well, I'm going to bed."

"Already?"

"Yes, I'm exhausted."

"See? I knew it."

"Knew what?"

"You don't love me any more, Delphine. You don't love me any more."

"Why do you say that?"

"You won't even argue with me."

"Is that what you think love is?"

"Yes. I just made all that stuff up to check—"

"What? You made it up?"

"Yes. I did bump into her, but we didn't go for a coffee together."

"I don't understand you. I don't know what's true any more."

"I just wanted to have an argument."

"An argument? You want me to smash a vase just to make you happy?"

"Why not?"

Delphine moved closer to Frédéric. "You're crazy." She was realizing the truth of this a little more every day. She'd known it wouldn't be easy to live with a writer. But she loved him; she loved him so much, and had done from the first second. So she said: "Do you want an argument, my love?"

"Yes."

"Not tonight, because I'm shattered. But soon, my love. Soon…"

And they both knew that she always kept her promises.

5

Delphine had hoped the book would be a success, she'd wanted it so badly that she couldn't sleep, but had she ever imagined a phenomenon like this? No, it wasn't possible. Her mind, though capable of the most extravagant dreams, could never have envisaged the improbable events that would follow.

It all began with a media frenzy. Journalists were immediately enraptured by the story of the novel, which they considered *amazing, incredible, extraordinary*. Hyperbole, of course, but our era has a love of facile exaggeration. Within a few days, Pick's novel was the toast of literary France. The novel, and the story behind it. For the newspapers, it was an exciting subject, a great story. One journalist, a friend of Delphine's, compared the phenomenon to Houellebecq's most recent book.

Delphine was surprised. "What makes you say that?"

"*Submission* is his biggest success. Bigger than his Goncourt winner. But it's his worst book. I almost fell asleep reading it. Frankly, for anyone who likes Houellebecq, it's a long way short of his other work. He has an exceptional gift for narrative, but in *Submission* there's hardly any story. And the few good pages, about sexuality or solitude, are just tired retreads of stuff he's written before."

"I think you're being very harsh."

"But everybody wanted to read it because the idea is absolutely brilliant. Within two days, the whole of France was talking about it. Someone even asked the president of France in an interview: 'Are you going to read Houellebecq's new novel?' In terms of promoting a book, it doesn't get much better than that. It's a polemic masquerading as a novel, it's remarkable."

"It's always like that, every time he brings out a book. People always go on about stuff that isn't even in his novels. Doesn't matter though. He's still a great writer."

"That's not the point. With *Submission*, he left the novel behind. He has entered a new era before anyone else. The text has no importance any more. What matters is having one very strong idea. An idea that will make people talk."

"What does that have to do with Pick?"

"It's less inflammatory, it's less brilliant, and it's not by a public relations genius, but everybody is talking about your book, and not because of the actual text. You could have published the IKEA catalogue and it would still have been a bestseller. The book itself isn't that good. It's slow in parts, it's kind of clichéd. The only really interesting bit is Pushkin dying. Basically, it's a novel about the absurd death of a poet."

Delphine didn't share the journalist's opinion. It was obvious that the fabulous commercial success of Pick's novel was linked to its context, but she didn't think that explained all of it. She'd heard from many readers who'd been deeply moved by the book. She herself thought it was excellent. But in one sense the journalist was right: people were talking much more about the mystery of Henri Pick than about his book. A huge number of journalists called her, trying to find out more about the dead pizzeria owner. Some even launched investigations into his life. Who was he? When did he write the book? And why hadn't he wanted to publish it? They wanted answers to all these questions. Soon, there would undoubtedly be new revelations about the author of *The Last Hours of a Love Affair*.

6

Success breeds success. When the novel had shifted 100,000 copies, many newspapers started writing about it again, using the word "phenomenon". Everybody wanted the first interview with "the widow". Until then, Delphine had thought it preferable to keep Madeleine in the shadows; to let people speculate about the backstory without too much information. Now that the book was a hit, they could launch a new publicity campaign around the discovery of the woman who had shared Henri Pick's life.

Delphine decided to let Madeleine appear on the television show *La Grande Librairie*. The presenter, François Busnel, had obtained an exclusive interview with her on the condition that filming took place in Crozon. Madeleine had no desire to go to a TV studio in Paris. Busnel often conducted interviews away from the French capital, but usually so he could meet a Paul Auster or a Philip Roth in the United States. All the same, he was happy to have this scoop; at last, the world would find out more about Henri Pick. After all, behind every male writer there is often a woman.

Delphine slept very badly the night before her departure for Brittany. In the middle of the night, she was jolted awake by a sort of convulsion. She asked Frédéric what had happened. "Nothing, my love," he replied. "Nothing happened." She couldn't fall back asleep, so she sat on the living-room sofa for the rest of the night, waiting for morning.

7

A few hours later, accompanied by a television camera crew, she rang the doorbell at Madeleine's house. The old lady hadn't imagined that so many people would come all this way to see her: there was even a make-up artist. She found this ridiculous. "I'm not Catherine Deneuve," she said. Delphine explained that everybody who appeared on television had to wear make-up, but it made no difference. Madeleine wanted to be natural, and perhaps it was better that way. The television crew quickly realized that this old Breton woman was not the kind of person to let herself be put upon. François Busnel tried to charm her with a few compliments about the décor of her living room, a task that required him to plumb the depths of his imagination. In the end, he understood that the best thing would be to talk about the region itself, Brittany. And he made a few references to Breton authors that Madeleine didn't know much about.

Filming began. Busnel started by talking about the genesis of the novel. His enthusiasm was real, without being excessive. Presenters of literary TV shows have to find a middle ground between the charisma necessary for TV shows generally and the subtlety preferred by a public who favour seriousness over theatricality. Finally, he addressed Madeleine: "Hello, madame."

"Call me Madeleine."

"Hello, Madeleine. May I ask you where we are?"

"But you know perfectly well where we are. What a weird question."

"It's for the viewers. I'd like you to introduce the location, because the programme usually takes place in Paris."

"Oh yes, everything takes place in Paris. Well, that's what the Parisians think."

"So… Here we are in…"

"My house. In Brittany. In Crozon."

Madeleine pronounced each sentence a little louder than the one before, as if her pride could only express itself in a rise in vocal volume.

Delphine, sitting behind the cameras, watched in surprise as the show began. Madeleine seemed astonishingly at ease, perhaps because she wasn't fully aware that hundreds of thousands of people would be watching her. How could you imagine so many people, after all, when only one man is talking to you? Busnel cut to the chase: "Apparently you had no idea that your husband had written a novel."

"That's right."

"Were you very surprised?"

"To start with, yes. I couldn't believe it. But Henri was unusual."

"In what way?"

"He didn't speak much. Maybe he was like that because he wanted to keep all his words for his book."

"He ran a pizzeria, correct?"

"Yes. Well, we did. The two of us."

"Of course, I'm sorry, you both ran it. So you were together every day. When could he have done his writing?"

"Probably in the mornings. Henri liked to go to work early. He'd get everything ready for the lunch shift, but I'm sure he had some spare time."

"There's no date on the manuscript. All we know is the year that it was delivered to the library. Perhaps he wrote it over a long period of time?"

"Perhaps. I have no way of knowing."

"And what did you think of the book?"

"It's a good story."

"Were you aware that he liked certain writers?"

"I never saw him read a book."

"Really? Never?"

"I'm a bit too old to start lying."

"And Pushkin? You found a book by the Russian poet in your house, is that right?"

"Yes. In the attic."

"To remind our viewers, your husband's novel describes the last hours of a love affair, a couple who have decided to separate, and also the death throes of Alexander Pushkin. An intense, gripping description of the poet's death, during which he suffered terribly."

"He certainly did a lot of moaning."

"It is 27th January 1837 and, if I may say so, he is unlucky not to be killed instantly. 'Life didn't want to escape him, preferring to remain inside a body and make it suffer', to quote your husband. He writes about the coagulating blood. This image recurs constantly, as the love between the two other characters becomes a dark blood. It's very beautiful."

"Thank you."

"So you found a book by Pushkin."

"Yes, I already told you that. Up in the attic. In a cardboard box."

"Had you ever seen that book before in your house?"

"No. Henri didn't read. Even with the newspaper, he just quickly leafed through it. He said it was always bad news."

"So what did he do with his spare time?"

"We didn't have much. We never went on holiday. He liked cycling, the Tour de France. Especially the Breton riders. He once saw Bernard Hinault in real life, and that put him in a state. I'd never seen him like that before. You had to get up pretty early to impress Henri."

"Yes, I imagine so… But let's return to *Yevgeny Onegin*, the book by Pushkin that was found in your attic. Your husband underlined a passage. I'd like to read it out, if you'll permit me."

"All right," said Madeleine.

François Busnel opened the book and read a few words:[11]

> To live and think is to be daunted,
> To feel contempt for other men.
> To feel is to be hurt, and haunted
> By days that will not come again,
> With a lost sense of charm and wonder,
> And memory to suffer under—
> The stinging serpent of remorse.
> This all adds piquancy, of course,
> To conversation.

After leaving a rather long silence, a rare event on a television show, the presenter asked: "Does that inspire anything in you?"

"No," Madeleine replied without hesitation.

"This passage is about a contempt for humanity. Your husband lived a very discreet life. He didn't try to have his novel published. Was this down to a desire not to mix with other people?"

"It's true that he was discreet. And he preferred us to stay home when we weren't working. But don't say that he didn't like people. He was never contemptuous of anybody."

11   He enunciated them with great slowness and power; it would be easy to imagine that he had been an actor in his youth.

"And what of that line about remorse? Did he have any regrets in his life?"

Madeleine, usually so talkative and quick to respond, seemed to hesitate before finally saying nothing. The silence deepened.

Busnel said: "Are you thinking about something in your life or would you prefer not to answer?"

"It's personal. You ask a lot of questions. Is this a television show or an interrogation?"

"It's just a television show, Madeleine, I promise you. We simply want to get to know you a little better, and your husband too. We would like to know what was hiding behind the author."

"I get the feeling he didn't want anybody to know."

"Do you think this book was personal? That the story might be partly autobiographical?"

"It was probably inspired by our separation, when we were seventeen. But after that, the story is very different. Maybe he heard the story in the restaurant. Some customers used to stay there all afternoon, drinking and talking about their lives. I once told my life story to a hairdresser, so I can understand that. Actually, can I say hello to him? He'd like that."

"Yes, of course."

"Then again, I don't know if he watches this. He's more a fan of cookery shows, you know."

"No problem. We can say hello to him anyway," said Busnel, flashing a complicit smile at the camera to share his amusement with the programme's viewers; unlike the shows that were filmed before a live studio audience, he had no way of knowing whether he had succeeded in establishing this rapport or whether his wink had fallen flat. But he had no desire to let the interview dwindle into trivia; he was determined to remain focused on his subject, and still hoped to discover some new or surprising information about Pick. Nobody could read this novel without being avidly curious about its improbable backstory. Our era is generally on the hunt for the truth behind everything, particularly fiction.

8

In order to maintain the viewer's interest until the end of the show, it was time to take a break. Usually, there was a brief interview at this point with a bookseller, who would share some of his current favourite books; but as this was a special edition of the show, another journalist had interviewed Magali Croze, hoping to find out more about the famous section of the library devoted to rejected books.

Since agreeing to the interview, Magali had been on the verge of despair. She'd bought some self-tanning pills at the pharmacy, which had turned her skin an unusual shade somewhere between faded yellow and carrot-orange. She had gone to her hairdresser (the same one to whom Madeleine had said hello) on three different occasions, each time choosing a new style before regretting her decision. In the end she opted for a strange fringe that made her forehead look exceptionally long. The hairdresser thought she looked *extraordinary*, a word he accompanied by placing his hands on his cheeks, as if he

himself were surprised at having been capable of such a creation. And perhaps he was: nobody in the history of hairdressing
had ever seen such a hairstyle before, a blend of the baroque
and the classical, the futuristic and the old-fashioned.

Next came her outfit. She quickly chose[12] to wear her pale-
pink suit. To her surprise, she struggled to fit inside it, but she
managed in the end, even at the risk of suffocation. With her
new complexion, her new haircut and that suit rescued from
the depths of her walk-in wardrobe, Magali barely recognized herself. José, her husband, who had grown thinner and
thinner while she grew fatter and fatter (as if the couple had
a fixed maximum weight which they had to share between
both bodies), stood transfixed as he looked at this new vision
of his wife. He thought of an overinflated pink balloon with
a cabbage-shaped head on top.

"What do you think?" she asked him.

"I don't know. It's… bizarre."

"Oh, why did I bother asking you? You don't know anything!"

The husband went off to the kitchen, leaving the storm
behind him. His wife had talked to him that way for a long
time now. They tended to exchange silences or shouts; very
rarely did their marriage produce a normal conversation.
How long had it been like that? It is difficult to pinpoint the
moment when love turns sour. It is gradual, insidious, a long
downward slide. Life had undergone a logistical change with

12   In fact, it was the only item of clothing she owned classy enough for
such an event.

the birth of their two boys, and they ascribed the increasing distance between them to the exhausting nature of their daily lives. Things will be better when the children have grown up, they thought; we'll be closer again then. But in fact it was quite the opposite. The boys' departure left a huge void behind; a sort of emotional cliff face in the living room. A giant crack that no tired relationship could ever hope to fill. The boys brought them life, subjects of conversation, engagement with the world. Now, none of that existed any more.

José, though, decided to go back and reassure his wife. "Everything will be fine."

"You think?"

"I know it. You'll be perfect."

Magali was touched by this sudden tenderness. She had to admit that their emotional relationship was difficult to define, constantly vacillating between black and white, and she no longer knew what to think of it. When she was angry, she wanted to break up with him; and then she loved him again, almost to her surprise.

Magali was also confused about the filmed interview. In fact, she hadn't really understood what it would be like. She'd prepared as if she was going to appear on the nine o'clock news. For her, "being on television" meant: "Everybody is going to see me". She hadn't realized that she would be part of a two-minute section largely composed of images of the library and the comments of various readers. All that effort just to sit in front of the cameras for seventeen seconds on a literary programme that, even if it beat its own record audience, would remain relatively obscure. The journalist asked her to describe how the idea for the library came about. She talked briefly about Jean-Pierre Gourvec and how enthusiastic she had been about his brilliant project:[13]

"Unfortunately, it wasn't the big success he hoped it would be. But since Monsieur Pick's book came out, things have changed. The library has far more visitors. People are so curious. I spot them as soon as they come in, the ones who are there to drop off their manuscript. Obviously, it's a lot more work for me…"

She was ready to keep talking for considerably longer, but the journalist abruptly thanked her for her "valuable insight". The journalist knew that his report would only be a short insert, so there was no point recording too much material; it would only complicate the editing process. Magali, disappointed, continued talking anyway, with or without the camera. "It's strange. Sometimes I have more than ten people at the same time. I've never seen anything like it. If it goes on like this, there'll be a bus full of Japanese tourists turning up any day now!" She smiled as she said this, but nobody was listening any more. She was right, though: the craze for the library would continue to grow. For now, Magali headed towards her small office and removed her make-up, with the same melancholy bitterness as an old actress in her dressing room after the last performance of a play.

13   A slight alteration of the truth, as anyone who read the beginning of this book will know.

9

The report on the library had been quickly edited so that Madeleine could see it during the recording of her interview. François Busnel asked her for a reaction.

"It's incredible to see everything that's happening here," she said. "I've heard that people are going to our old pizzeria just to see where my husband might have written his book. Anyway, I hope they don't go there wanting to eat pizza, because it's a crêperie now."

"How do you feel about all this enthusiasm?"

"I don't really understand it. It's just a book."

"Readers are naturally curious, though. That's also why there are so many journalists investigating your husband's past."

"Yes, I know, everybody wants to talk to me. They're rummaging through our lives, and I don't like that. I was advised to talk to you. I hope you're pleased. Because if I say what I think, I hope the others will leave me in peace. Some of them have been visiting his grave, and they don't even know him. That's not a good thing to do. He was my husband. I'm glad people are reading his book, but... well, that's enough now."

Madeleine pronounced these last words in a firm voice. Nobody was expecting it, but this was how she felt. She didn't like the whole circus that had grown up around her husband. François Busnel had mentioned the journalists investigating Pick's life: would there be revelations? Some of them were driven by a different kind of impulse. Several[14] believed that the pizzeria owner could not have written a novel. They didn't know who had written it, or why the author had used Pick's name, but they felt certain the facts were there, just waiting to be discovered. Madeleine's interview, confirming her husband's dull and uncultured life, only supported their hunch. Each of them would do whatever it took to find the key to this mystery. The race was on.

10

The day after the programme was broadcast, the viewing figures were released. Everybody was amazed. It was historical, record-breaking. Such figures for a literary television show had not been seen in years, since Bernard Pivot presented *Apostrophes*. A few days later, the book went to number one on the bestseller list. Even sales of Pushkin went up. The craze spread beyond France, with increasingly high offers for translation rights, particularly from Germany. In a context of economic crisis and geopolitical instability, Madeleine's sincerity, allied to the miracle of the manuscript's history, had laid the foundations for a massive international success.

14 Among them, Jean-Michel Rouche, a former journalist at *Figaro Littéraire*, specializing in German literature (he was a hardcore fan of the Mann family), who—after being fired from his job—was now trying to scrape a living as a freelancer, writing puff pieces and presenting literary events. For now, he is no more than a footnote, but soon he will become a major character in this story.

In Crozon, this media frenzy changed the way people looked at Madeleine. In the market, she could tell that people's attitudes towards her were no longer the same. They watched her as if she were a fairground freak, and she found herself smiling at everyone to cover her embarrassment. The town's mayor offered to organize a small party in her honour, but she categorically refused. She'd agreed to let her husband's novel be published, she'd agreed to appear on a television programme, but that was the end of it. It was out of the question that her life should change. (It was far from certain that she was the one to decide that.)

Faced with Madeleine's desire for privacy, the journalists decided to fall back on the writer's daughter. Joséphine, after years lurking in the shadows, considered this sudden fascination with her as something of a godsend. Life was offering her a chance for revenge. When Marc left her, she'd felt that nobody would be interested in her ever again, but now here she was, centre stage. The journalists wanted to know what her father was like, if he used to tell her stories when she was a little girl. If it went on like this, they'd soon be asking her if she preferred broccoli or aubergine. Like a briefly famous reality-TV star, she was seduced by the idea of being special. *Ouest-France* sent a journalist to conduct a full-length interview. Joséphine couldn't believe it. "The most widely read newspaper in France," she sighed. When they took pictures, she asked them to use her shop as a backdrop. By the next day, sales of her lingerie had doubled. People queued up to buy a bra from the daughter of the pizzeria owner who'd written a novel in absolute secrecy (one of the bizarre paths taken by this particular form of posthumous fame).

Joséphine had regained the use of her zygomatic muscles. Now she could be seen parading outside her shop, looking like a lottery winner. In conversation with interviewers, she rewrote her own life story: she talked about how close she had been to her father, she lied that she had always sensed some mysterious inner life behind his calm facade. In the end she admitted what everybody wanted to hear: she wasn't surprised by what had been discovered. She passed over in silence (or had completely forgotten) her first reaction. She discovered a taste for the drug that is fame; each day, she wanted to spend even longer soaking up the limelight, to let it consume her.

She was also stunned to receive a phone call from Marc. He'd called her a few times after their separation, before vanishing completely from her life. For months on end, she would stare at the telephone, waiting for it to ring, for Marc to tell her that he'd made a terrible mistake. Some days, she would turn her mobile off and on again dozens of times to make sure it was working properly, even lifting it above her head in a ridiculous attempt to find better reception. But he had never called again. How was it possible for someone to break so completely with such a big part of their past? True, their most recent discussions had been little more than a chaotic succession of reproaches (her) and attempts to change the subject (him), and it was obvious that talking to each other equated to hurting each other.

They say that time heals, but some wounds remain open. She still missed Marc. Not only his presence in bed in the mornings, but even his faults: the way he used to grunt instead of saying "yes" or "no", or sometimes even "maybe". Joséphine loved what she had previously hated. She thought about their first meeting, about the birth of their daughters. All those images of happiness, ruined by that untimely end. The moment when he said: "We need to talk." That famous, hopeless phrase that actually means: there is nothing more to say. So it was over. But then the telephone in the shop started to ring. It was Marc, wanting to know how she was. Frozen in surprise, she said nothing. He went on: "I was wondering if I could see you, have a coffee together, if that's okay with you?" Yes, it really was Marc speaking. It was Marc asking her if she was okay with seeing him again. She gathered her scrambled thoughts and said: "Yes." She wrote down the time and place of their meeting, then hung up. For several minutes, she stared at the telephone.

PART SIX

I

THE BOOK CONTINUED to top the bestseller lists, becoming a phenomenon with several unexpected consequences. The translation rights, naturally, were bought by publishers in many different countries, and the book was already a hit in Germany after being published in record time. The magazine *Der Spiegel* devoted a very long article to the novel, comparing Pick with other reclusive writers such as J.D. Salinger and Thomas Pynchon. The article even mentioned Julien Gracq, who refused to accept the Prix Goncourt in 1951 for his novel *The Opposing Shore*. The situation was not quite the same, but the general thesis of the article was that Pick belonged to a large subset of writers who want to be read without being seen. In the United States, the novel would come out under the title *The Unwanted Book*: a surprising choice, since it referred more to the story of the book's publication than the text itself, but tangible proof that our era was edging towards a complete domination of form over substance.

There were also several bids for the film rights, though nothing had yet been signed. Thomas Langmann, the producer of *The Artist*, began thinking about a film based not on the novel but on the author's life; he kept repeating to anyone who would listen: "It'll be a *biopick*!" For the moment, however, it was difficult to envisage a screenplay on that subject, because there was too much missing information, particularly concerning the circumstances in which Pick wrote his book. You couldn't make a two-hour film about a guy who makes pizzas and writes in the mornings when nobody else is around. "There are limits to contemplative cinema. This story would have been perfect for Antonioni, with Alain Delon and Monica Vitti in the starring roles..." Langmann daydreamed. In the end, he did not take up the option. Heidi Warneke, the warm-voiced German lady who runs the rights department at Grasset, continued to consider various offers without coming to a decision. It was better to wait for the right project than to rush into something; with the book's success continuing to grow, it was obvious that a bigger, better offer would be made very soon. Heidi secretly dreamt of Roman Polanski, whom she considered the only director capable of making a gripping film about a man shut up in a room. The book was a story about a blockage, about the impossibility of love between two people, and the director of *The Pianist* had a unique talent for filming physical and mental constriction. But he had just started shooting his new film, the story of a young German painter who was killed in Auschwitz.

2

There were yet other consequences, even more unexpected. Some people began to embrace the good fortune of being rejected. Publishers were not always right; Pick was further proof of that. These people conveniently forgot that there was no evidence that Pick had actually sent his manuscript to any publishers. But it was a wave that could be surfed. With the rise of digital publishing, more and more writers were putting their books directly online after being rejected by traditional publishers. And the public could make such books a success, as was the case with Anna Todd's *After* series.

Richard Ducousset at Albin Michel was the first person to transform this trend into a marketing idea. He asked his assistant to find a few books that were "not too bad" among the pile of recently rejected novels. After all, publishers sometimes think about publishing a novel, then decide against it despite the book possessing certain qualities. The assistant called the selected author to find out how many rejections he'd received.

"You're calling me to find out how many other publishers rejected my book?"

"Yes."

"That's weird."

"We'd just like to know."

"About ten, I think."

"Thank you very much," she said, hanging up.

Ten wasn't enough. They needed to find a champion of rejection. The eventual winner was Gustave Horn, who wrote a novel called *My Brother's Glory*, rejected by thirty-two different publishers. Richard Ducousset immediately offered a contract to the author, who initially thought it was a prank. Was there a hidden camera somewhere? But no, the contract was real.

"I don't understand this. A few months ago, you didn't want my book. You sent me a standard rejection letter."

"We changed our mind," the editor explained. "Everybody makes mistakes…"

A few weeks later, the book came out with a sticker on the cover announcing proudly: "A novel rejected thirty-two times."

This book did not replicate Pick's success, but it did sell more than 20,000 copies, which is pretty impressive. Readers were intrigued by the idea of a novel rejected that many times. There was something transgressive about this attraction. Incapable of perceiving the irony of the situation, Gustave Horn felt that his talent had finally been rewarded. He was baffled when his publisher turned down his next manuscript.

3

Jack Lang, the former French minister of culture, had the idea of establishing an Unpublished Authors Day,[15] when the country would recognize all those who wrote without reward. From its first year, the day was a popular success. In a similar vein to the Festival of Music, also created by Lang, the budding novelists and poets of France filled the streets to read out their stories and share their words with anyone who would listen.

15 He did consider calling it something simpler, such as "Writing Day" or "The Festival of Writing". But, in the end, he preferred to emphasise unpublished authors: it was a way not of celebrating amateurism but of empowering writers who had not received public recognition.

An investigation by the newspaper *Le Parisien* confirmed that one French person in three wanted to write: "One can almost say today that there are more writers than readers," concluded Pierre Vavasseur in his article. On RTL Radio, Bernard Lehut chronicled the success of Unpublished Authors Day and noted: "We all have a Pick inside of us." The success of that book, discovered amid other rejects, spoke to the yearnings of an entire population who hungered to be read. For the occasion, Augustin Trapenard interviewed a Hungarian philosopher whose specialization was the question of erasure, notably in the work of Maurice Blanchot. But there was a problem: this man was so intensely engaged with his subject that he kept leaving interminable silences between his sentences, as if he wished to gradually erase himself from the airwaves.

So Pick was on everybody's lips, a symbol of the dream that one day, *you too* would be recognized for your talent. Of course, some people claim to write only for themselves, but how can anyone believe that? Words always have a destination; they aspire to be read by other eyes. Writing for yourself would be like packing your suitcase and then not going anywhere. While readers did enjoy Pick's novel, it was above all the story behind it that moved them. It echoed the fantasy of being somebody else, the unsuspected superhero, the ordinary-seeming man whose secret is that he possesses an imperceptible literary sensibility. And the less people knew about him, the more fascinating he was. There was nothing to his biography beyond the straight line of a banal, boring life. This fanned the flames of admiration; it added to his myth. Increasing numbers of readers went in search of his tracks, visited his grave. The cemetery in Crozon was filled with his most fervent fans. Madeleine would sometimes see them there. Unable to understand what they wanted, she had no hesitation in asking them to leave her husband in peace. Was she the kind of person who thought it was possible to wake the dead? In any case, you could stir up their secrets.

These unusual visitors also went to the Picks' pizzeria. They were disappointed to find that it was now a crêperie. The new owners, Gérard Misson and his wife Nicole, surprised by the crowds converging on their humble restaurant, decided to add pizzas to the menu. The first few days were disastrous; the *crêpier* struggled to make the transition. "I have to make pizzas now… and all because of a book," he kept repeating incredulously, as he tried to familiarize himself with the pizza oven. Soon, there were no more crêpes. As more and more customers came to visit the cellar where Pick had written his novel, Misson warmed to his new vocation, organizing pilgrimages and inventing stories that, over the months that followed, became increasingly elaborate. So it was that the novel of the novel wrote itself.

One morning, while he was making an inventory of his storeroom, Gérard Misson decided to bring down one of the tables from the restaurant. He took a chair, and sat down to write. This man, who had never written a line in his life, thought that inspiration might strike if he sat in this magical place with a sheet of paper and a biro in his hand. But nothing happened. Not a single idea. Not the merest hint of an opening sentence. On the whole, he thought, it was easier to make crêpes (or even pizzas). He was terribly disappointed, having spent several days daydreaming about becoming a successful writer.

His wife found him in that improbable position.

"What are you doing?"

"It... it's not what you think."

"Are you writing? You?"

Nicole laughed, and went back up to the restaurant. She had not meant to mock him, but her husband felt humiliated. Evidently his wife did not believe him capable of writing, or even just sitting and thinking. They never spoke about the incident again, but it was the beginning of the end of their marriage. Sometimes you have to do something surprising, drift away from the current of daily life, to find out what your partner really thinks of you.

4

The break-up of the Missons' marriage was one of the many unforeseen consequences of the publication of Pick's novel. This novel changed lives. And, of course, the book's fame spread to the library of rejects from which it had been plucked.

Magali, who hadn't really thought about it in years, had to reorganize the space devoted to the books that the publishing industry had forsaken. To start with, there was only a trickle of new arrivals, but soon after that it became a flood.

It seemed that every person in France had a manuscript tucked away. Many of them didn't realize that they were supposed to come in person to deposit their book; dozens of novels started arriving by post every day, as if the little library were a Parisian publishing house. Overwhelmed by the situation, Magali asked for help from the mayor's office, which opened an annexe to the library, devoted exclusively to rejected books. Crozon became the capital of France's unpublished authors.

It was strange to see this remote little town, usually so quiet, invaded by all these human shadows, these men and women driven by love of the written word. It was easy to spot those who had come to drop off their manuscript. But not all of them looked defeated. Some people thought it chic to leave a text here, even a private journal. The town welcomed everybody's words, a baroque overflow of sentences. Sometimes, the writers came from far away; two Poles travelled from Cracow just to deliver what they believed to be a misunderstood masterpiece.

One young man, Jérémie, came from south-west France to abandon a collection of short stories and poems that he had written over the previous few months. About twenty years old, he looked like Kurt Cobain: lanky and stoop-shouldered, with long, blond, dirty hair; but a strange light seemed to emanate from this scruffy exterior. Jérémie was a throwback to another age, like a photograph from a 1970s high school yearbook come to life. His writing was influenced by René Char and Henri Michaux. His poetry, while attempting to be political and intellectual, was above all completely obscure to everyone but its author. Jérémie was fragile in the way of those people who cannot find their place in the world, and who wander endlessly searching for a place to lay their head.

Magali was tired of constantly welcoming these manuscript-bearers, and she sometimes cursed Gourvec for his hare-brained idea. More than ever, she considered the project absurd, seeing it only as a massive added workload. When she first spotted Jérémie, she assumed he was just another lost soul, rejected by the world, who had come here to buttonhole her like all the others. In fact, he smiled as he presented her with his manuscript. His sweet attitude made an interesting clash with his wild, rugged appearance. In the end, she decided she liked him. And not only that, but she thought him extremely handsome.

"I'm trusting you not to read my manuscript," he said, almost whispering. "It's very private, you see."

"No, don't worry…" Magali replied, blushing slightly.

Jérémie knew that this woman would read what he'd written, precisely because of what he'd just said. That didn't matter. This place was like an island where the idea of being judged had no importance. Here, he felt lighter. Usually very shy, despite his apparent self-confidence, he stayed a moment in the library to observe Magali. Discomfited by those blue eyes gazing at her, she tried to look busy. But it was obvious that she had been basically accomplishing nothing since he arrived. Why was he looking at her like that? Could he be a psychopath? No, he seemed quite gentle, harmless. You could tell from the way he walked, spoke, breathed; as if he were apologizing for existing. Yet he had an undeniable charisma. It was impossible to stop looking at this man who acted like a ghost.[16]

He stood there a little longer without speaking. Occasionally they smiled at each other. Finally he went up to Magali.

"Could we maybe go out for a drink? After you finish work?"

"A drink?"

"Yes, I'm on my own here. I came a long way to bring my manuscript. I don't know anybody... So, it'd be nice if you could."

"All right," said Magali, surprising herself with this spontaneous reply that had not been authorized by her rational mind. But she'd said yes now, so... she would go for a drink with him. It was just out of politeness; he didn't know anybody. And that was the only reason he wanted to go for a drink with her, of course. He didn't want to be alone. It's perfectly understandable; yes, that's why he wants to go for a drink with me, thought Magali, brooding obsessively over the situation.

5

A few minutes later, she sent her husband a text: she was busy at work, so she would be late home. This was the first time she had ever lied to him; not out of principle, but simply because

16 If Magali had known Pasolini, she might have thought of his film *Teorema*, where the central character makes souls tremble with the simple power of his ghostlike presence.

she'd never needed to tell him anything but the truth before. The problem was that Crozon was a small town where everybody knew one another. The best thing, perhaps, would be to stay inside the library, after closing. She had an office there where they could have a drink. Why had she said yes? She felt magnetized by the moment. If she backed out now, she had the feeling that nothing else would ever happen in her life. Hadn't she dreamt of this? It was hard for her to know exactly what she was feeling. She hadn't thought about her desires, or even her sexuality, in such a long time. Her husband barely touched her these days; sometimes, when he was aroused, he would relieve himself mechanically inside her; it wasn't necessarily unpleasant, but it was all fairly basic, without any hint of sensuality. And now this young man wanted to have a drink with her. How old was he? He looked younger than her sons. Maybe twenty? She hoped he wasn't younger. That would be sordid. But she wasn't going to ask him. She didn't want to know anything about him, in fact, preferring to leave the moment mysterious, a non-reality that would have no effect on the rest of her life. Anyway, they were only going to have a drink. Yes, that was all: just a drink.

He was finishing his beer now, and staring at her. She turned her face away, trying to regain some composure. She uttered a few phrases, meaningless words, anything to break this unbearable silence. Jérémie asked her to relax: there was no obligation to talk. They could just sit here in silence. That was fine with him. He was opposed to all conventions in relationships, the first and most important being the obligation to talk when there are two of you. Despite that, he started a conversation:

"It's a strange library."

"Strange?"

"Yeah, it's weird, don't you think, this collection of rejected books? Like a cursed place or something."

"It wasn't my idea."

"So, what do you think of it?"

"For me, it had ceased to exist. And then Pick's book came out…"

"You really think he was the one who wrote it?"

"Yes, of course. Why wouldn't it have been him?"

"I dunno. You make pizzas, you never read a book, and after your death it turns out you wrote a great novel. It just seems weird, doesn't it?"

"I don't know."

"Do *you* do things that nobody knows about?"

"No…"

"So whose idea was it, this library?"

"The man who hired me. Jean-Pierre Gourvec."

"Did he write?"

"I don't know. I didn't know him that well."

"How much time did you spend with him?"

"Just over ten years."

"You were with him every day for ten years, in this tiny little place, and you say you didn't know him?"

"Yes, well… I mean, we talked. But I was never really sure what he was thinking."

"Do you think you'll read my book?"

"I don't think so. Unless you want me to. I never open any of the books that are deposited here. They're often pretty bad, it has to be said. Everybody thinks they're a writer these days. And it's been even worse since Pick's success. To hear them speak, everybody you meet is a misunderstood genius. Well, that's what they all tell me. I get lumbered with so many losers…"

"What about me?"

"What about you?"

"What did you think of me when you saw me?"

"…"

"You don't want to tell me?"

"I thought you were very handsome."

Magali couldn't quite believe she was talking like this. Simply. Frankly. She might easily have been embarrassed by the probing nature of their discussion, but she wasn't; she wanted to keep talking with him, to drink until morning, hoping that the night would never end, that the sun would never rise on a new day, that they would lose themselves somewhere in a time warp. She was an honest, straightforward person, but she never talked about her feelings or emotions. Why had she admitted that she found him handsome? Because it was her main thought, squeezing out all the others. She could enjoy talking to him, but the enjoyment was minor compared to the physical desire that was slowly overcoming her. How long was it since she'd felt this way? She had no idea. Perhaps it was the first time she'd ever felt it. This desire was as intense as the erotic void that had preceded it. Jérémie stared at her, a faint smile on his lips, as if he were taking pleasure in slowing time down, in not rushing into anything.

Finally he stood up and walked over to her. He put his head on her shoulder. She tried to control her breathing, hoping that he couldn't sense the incredible pounding of her heart. Jérémie moved his hand along Magali's body, lifting up her dress; he slid his finger inside her before he even kissed her. She clung to him desperately; the simple fact of being touched had sent her into a forgotten world. He kissed her passionately, holding her neck firmly with his hand; she tipped backwards, as light as if her body were evaporating with pleasure. He took her hand and moved it towards his penis; she touched it clumsily, without looking, but he was already hard. He told her to stand up and turn around, and then he took her from behind. It was impossible for Magali to guess how long it lasted; each second erased the previous one in a physical pleasure so intense even the present was forgotten.

6

The two of them were lying on the floor now, in darkness, Magali with her dress lifted up, Jérémie with his trousers pulled down. She heard her phone ringing—probably her husband—but that didn't matter. She hoped she could make love again that evening, suddenly incredulous that she had spent her whole life deprived of the presence of other bodies. But she got dressed, feeling embarrassed at being half naked like that. How could he have desired her? And why her? He could probably have any woman he wanted. It was like a mirage, or the kind of thing that only happens in films. She mustn't get carried away, just savour the beauty of the moment; he would leave, and it would be perfect; she could live and relive every second of the memory in her mind, and that would enable it to exist again.

"Why are you getting dressed?"

"I don't know."

"Do you have to go home? Is your husband expecting you?"

"No. Well, yes."

"I'd like you to stay, if you can. I'll probably spend the night here, if you're okay with that. I don't have a hotel room."

"Yes, of course."

"I want you again."

"You don't think I'm too…"

"Too what?"

"You don't think I'm too fat?"

"No, not at all. I like women with curves. It's reassuring."

"Did you need that much reassurance?"

"…"

7

José, becoming anxious, sent another message: he was coming to the library. Magali replied, apologizing for getting caught up with the inventory and saying she was on her way home.

She gathered all her belongings and stuffed them at random into her bag, casting quick glances at the man she'd just made love with.

"So I'm an inventory," he sighed.

"I have to go home. I have no choice."

"Don't worry, I understand."

"Will you be here tomorrow morning?" Magali asked, although she already knew the answer. He was going to leave; he was the kind of man who left. Yet he replied, with intense conviction in his voice, that he would be there; he sounded very sure. He kissed her one last time, without saying anything. But Magali had the feeling that she'd heard words. Had he spoken? Her senses were confused, leading to these little hallucinations where she had to hold tight to her lover to be certain of reality. At last, he whispered: "Tomorrow morning, come before the library opens, and wake me with your mouth…" Magali didn't try to understand the precise meaning of this erotic request, she just let herself be flooded by the happiness inspired by this carnal rendezvous; in a few hours, they would be together again.

She got in the car and, although she knew she ought to hurry home, just sat there in suspense for a while. She turned on the lights, then started the engine. Each insignificant gesture took on quasi-mythological proportions, as if what had just happened was spreading throughout her life. Even the way back home, which she'd driven every day for decades, seemed different.

PART SEVEN

I

A FEW YEARS AGO, Jean-Michel Rouche was a man with real influence in literary circles. His articles were feared, particularly his column in *Figaro Littéraire*. He enjoyed this power, playing hard to get when press officers asked to meet him for lunch, always leaving a dramatic pause before giving his opinion on this or that novel, knowing that his voice would echo like an oracle. He was the prince of an ephemeral kingdom that he imagined eternal. All it took was the appointment of a new editor at the newspaper, and he was sacked. Another writer wore his crown before, in turn, being dismissed a few years later; such was the ceaseless waltz of fragile power.

Without realizing it, Rouche had made a lot of enemies during his glory years. He hadn't thought that he was being mean or unfair, just intellectually honest about what he felt, bravely denouncing pretentiousness and overrated writers. He hadn't always acted in a career-minded way; nobody could accuse him of that. But now it was impossible for him to find an outlet to express himself; not on radio, not on television, and certainly not in the press. Gradually, he would be forgotten; anyone who tried to remember his name would say, "Oh, hang on, it's on the tip of my tongue…"

However, the hellish period he was going through had not made him bitter, but almost kindly. He presented round-table discussions in provincial towns, and came to realize that behind every writer, even the most mediocre, there was a will to work, the dream of accomplishing something. He shared cold buffets and hand-rolled cigarettes with the witnesses of his decline. In the evenings, in his hotel room, he would examine his hair, observing with horror as it gradually, inexorably disappeared. Particularly from the top of his head. He drew a parallel between his social life and his baldness. The pattern was clear: he had begun to lose his hair on the day he was fired.

As soon as Pick's novel came out, Rouche developed a sort of obsession with the story behind it. Brigitte, his girlfriend of three years, didn't understand why he kept talking about this publication, which struck him as shady in some way. He scented a literary hoax.

"You see plots everywhere," said Brigitte.

"I don't believe an artist really wants to remain hidden. Well, I mean, it happens, but it's very rare."

"That's not true. Lots of people have a talent that they prefer to keep to themselves. Me, for example. Did you know that I sing in the shower?" Brigitte asked, very proud of this semi-sonic, semi-liquid repartee.

"No, I didn't know. And no offence, but I don't think that's quite the same thing."

"…"

"Listen, I just have a hunch about this. When I uncover the truth, a lot of people will be surprised, believe me."

"Well, I think it's a great story and I believe it. You're just cynical, and that's sad."

Jean-Michel didn't know how to respond to this somewhat brutal put-down. He could tell that Brigitte was growing tired of him. This didn't shock him. He was losing his hair, putting on weight, his social life was dull, and he was earning less money; he could no longer ask her out to a restaurant on a whim. He had to plan all his expenses in advance.

In fact, none of that really mattered to Brigitte. What she missed most of all was the passion of their early days; the way he would tell stories, his enthusiasm. Most of the time, he was still gentle and attentive, but she could feel his dark side gaining ground. He was being eaten up by bitterness. She wasn't surprised that he should be incredulous about that Breton author. And yet she was wrong. The truth was almost the exact opposite of what she thought. Something in Jean-Michel was awakening. It had been a long time since he'd felt this motivated. He wanted to investigate the story, and he felt convinced that the outcome would be crucial for his career. Thanks to Pick, he would return to the forefront of the literary scene. He needed to follow his intuition to find evidence of the fraud. His first move was to travel to Brittany.

He begged Brigitte to lend him her car. She was hesitant, because she knew he was a bad driver. But she wasn't against the idea of him going away for a few days. It might do them both some good. So she agreed, reminding him to be very careful, because she didn't have enough money to pay for additional insurance. He quickly packed his bag and got behind the wheel. Barely two hundred metres later, misjudging the first bend, he scraped the side of the Volvo.

2

After seeing Madeleine on television, Rouche felt convinced that there was no more information to be had from her. He had to focus on the daughter, who was much more expansive in her interviews. For now, she had only been asked to recount anecdotes about the past, but Rouche would do everything he could to persuade her to show him as many documents as possible. He felt sure that, somewhere, he would find proof that his intuition was correct. Joséphine was not getting weary of the media attention. She used it to talk about her shop, and the publicity she gained from it was considerable. Rouche had read the articles on the internet, and couldn't help having a negative opinion about her; in fact, he thought she was probably a bit stupid.

Driving to Rennes on the motorway, he obsessed over the scratch on the car. Brigitte was going to take it very badly. He could always deny responsibility. He could say he'd found the car in that state; that someone had scraped her car and hadn't even left a phone number. Case closed. It was perfectly plausible. But he felt sure that she wouldn't believe him. He was exactly the kind of man who scratches a borrowed car. He could promise to get it fixed, but how would he pay for it? The precariousness of his finances complicated all his relationships with other people. It was why he'd had to borrow a car in the first place. If he'd had enough money, he'd have been able to rent one—and to insure it up to the hilt.

As he drove, he thought about the last few months. He wondered where the spiral of failure would take him next. He had left his bourgeois apartment and now lived in an attic room in a chic Parisian apartment building; at least the address allowed him to keep up appearances. Nobody else would know that he had to take the emergency stairs instead of the lift. The only person he'd admitted the truth to was Brigitte. After several weeks of being together, he had not been able to hide the reality from her any longer. During those weeks, he'd refused to invite her to his place, to the point where she'd begun to suspect that he was married. She was actually relieved to discover the truth: Jean-Michel was broke. That didn't matter to her. She had brought up her son on her own, and had never relied on anyone else. When she found out the truth, Brigitte smiled: she always fell for skint men. But as the months passed, it became an inconvenience.

As he approached Rennes, Rouche tried to forget about the scratch and all the problems in his life, and to focus on his investigation. He felt alive as he drove; sometimes, you have to let a landscape unfold before your eyes in order to be certain that you exist. Obviously, he wasn't investigating a murder or a series of disappearances in Mexico,[17] but he did have to

17 He was in the middle of reading Roberto Bolaño's *2666*.

uncover a massive literary fraud. As he hadn't driven for a long time, he decided to take a break. Finally feeling happy, he drank a beer at a petrol station, and thought about buying a chocolate bar. In the end, he opted for another beer instead. He had promised himself that he would drink less, but this was no ordinary day.

It was mid-afternoon when Rouche arrived in Rennes. Without GPS, it took him another hour to find Joséphine's shop. He found a parking space just in front of it: for him, this was more a symbol than a concrete fact. He couldn't quite believe it. That empty parking space gave him a disproportionate feeling of joy. For years, every time he happened to drive, he would spend ages searching for somewhere to park before finally pulling up in a space reserved for deliveries, which left him stressed out all evening. Today, everything was different. Rendered quite emotional by this new order of things, he messed up his parallel parking and scratched the car again.

His joy quickly faded and the reality of his depressing condition stared him in the face. Now there was no way he'd be able to persuade Brigitte that it wasn't his fault. The likelihood of being hit by strangers twice in the same day was pretty low. Unless he invented a malicious enemy: someone who'd deliberately vandalized his car because of his investigation. He wasn't sure he could judge the credibility of this scenario. Why would anybody want to warn him off the investigation of a phantom author hiding behind a dead Breton pizzeria owner?

3

To give himself courage before taking the first step in his investigation, Rouche decided to go for a beer in the bar across the street. After finishing the first one, he immediately ordered its *little sister*, an expression dear to the hearts of French drinkers who hide the reality of their spiralling alcoholism under this sweet and tenderly ironic phrase.

A few minutes later, he went into the shop. He looked more like an old pervert there to ogle the lacy knickers than a romantic husband intending to buy his wife a gift. Mathilde, the new salesgirl, walked over to him. Despite a master's degree in business, she'd had great trouble finding steady employment. After a series of temporary jobs, she'd finally been given a permanent contract. She owed this stroke of luck to Henri Pick. The media frenzy around the book had provided so much publicity for Joséphine's lingerie shop that she'd had to hire an assistant. As it happens, Mathilde had read *The Last Hours of a Love Affair* and found it very sad. But she was the kind of person who cries easily.

"Hello, how may I help you?" she asked Rouche.

"I'd like to talk to Joséphine. I'm a journalist."

"I'm sorry, she isn't here."

"When will she be back?"

"I'm not sure. But not today, I think."

"You think or you know?"

"She said she was leaving for a while."

"That's pretty vague. Could you call her?"

"I already tried. She's not answering."

"That's strange. A few days ago, she was all over the press."

"No, it's not strange. She warned me in advance. I think she just needs a break."

"A break," he muttered to himself. This sudden disappearance struck him as very odd.

At that moment, a woman in her fifties entered the shop. The salesgirl asked her what she wanted, but she didn't reply. Blushing, she glanced at Rouche. He realized that he was responsible for her silence. Clearly, this woman had no desire to talk about her lingerie needs in front of him. He quickly thanked Mathilde and left the shop. Not knowing what else to do, he sat down at the terrace of the bar across the street.

4

At the same moment, Delphine and Frédéric were finishing a long lunch. She'd worked so hard recently that she was finally taking some time for herself—and for *her favourite author*. He had criticized her for spending less time with him, although that didn't mean that he didn't enjoy those solitary periods (one of his many paradoxes). According to Frédéric, being part of a couple was not just about spending time together.

Delphine was concentrating on her career. She received more and more phone calls these days from people congratulating her or trying to headhunt her. Other publishers saw her as one of those editorial geniuses who have a natural talent for sniffing out successful books and trends before everyone else. Sometimes she felt embarrassed at being the centre of all this attention; eventually, she felt, people would realize that she was still a little girl and her cover would be blown. For now, though, Henri Pick's book was closing in on sales of 300,000, a figure that far surpassed anybody's hopes.

"In ten days, Grasset is throwing a party to celebrate Pick's success," Delphine announced.

"Well, they're certainly not going to throw a party for my book, given how low its sales were."

"It will come. I'm sure you'll win a prize for your next novel."

"It's nice of you to say so. But I'm not from Brittany, I don't make pizzas and, worst of all, I'm alive."

"Stop it…"

"It took me two years to write my last book. I must have sold about 1,200 copies, including my family, my friends, and the books that I bought myself to give as presents. And then there are all those customers who bought it by accident. And the passers-by who took pity on me when I was doing a signing in a bookshop. In fact, if you only take real sales into account, I've probably sold a grand total of two books," he concluded with a smile.

She couldn't help laughing. Delphine had always liked Frédéric's self-mockery, even if it sometimes verged on bitterness.

"Meanwhile, this farce just gets bigger," he went on. "Did you see that several publishers are sending interns to Crozon? They're hoping to discover another hidden genius. When you think about the hopelessly crap books that we saw there, it really is a joke."

"Let them waste their time. It doesn't matter. What I care about is your next book."

"Actually, I wanted to tell you that I've got the title."

"You're kidding? That's great news!"

"…"

"So what are you waiting for? Tell me!"

"It's going to be called *The Man Who Told the Truth*."

Delphine looked into Frédéric's eyes but said nothing. Didn't she like it? In the end she stammered something about it being difficult to judge a title until you'd read the book. Frédéric promised that she would soon be able to read it.

A few minutes later, he asked her to take the afternoon off. As on their first date, he wanted to go for a walk with her, and then make love. Delphine pretended to hesitate (and that is probably what he most hated), then announced that she had too much work, especially with the party to organize. He didn't insist (and that is probably what she wanted him to do) and they separated in the middle of the street with a peck on the cheek that was supposed to contain the promise of a deeper, more intense kiss to come. Frédéric watched her leave, staring at her back in the hope that she would turn around. He daydreamed that she would give him one last sign, a gesture that he could take with him while he waited for their next encounter. But she didn't turn around.

5

Rouche spent the afternoon on the terrace of the bar, numbing himself with beer after beer. His investigation had begun with a dead end and he didn't know what to do. The night before, he had imagined himself as the bold knight of French literature, and it had given him the feeling that his life was finally becoming worthwhile again. But he had run into an uncooperative reality. Joséphine was nowhere in the vicinity, and nobody knew when she would return. He couldn't dismiss himself as a mediocre investigator, because he hadn't even had the chance to get started; he was a racing driver whose car had broken down on the starting line.[18] For years now, everything had been collapsing beneath his feet, and there was nothing he could do about it: fate continued to conspire against him. Alcohol tends to provoke either an enthusiasm of variable lucidity or a series of dark, pathetic visions. The liquid you consume finds itself at a crossroads in your body, and it has to choose; inside Rouche, it had chosen the negative path, enlivened with a hint of self-deprecation.

Thankfully, he'd just received an email from the Grasset press department inviting him to a party to celebrate Pick's success. He'd found it quite funny, reading that message while he was trying to track down what he suspected to be a hoax; but that was not his principal feeling. The main sensation

18   A strange mechanical analogy, given that the only notable events since his departure from Paris were the two scrapes he'd had with the car.

the email gave him was a simple happiness at being on the guest list, since this meant that he had not been completely forgotten. Month by month, he had been invited to fewer and fewer such occasions; the end of his power had entailed the end of his social life. He was no longer invited out to lunch, and certain press officers with whom he'd imagined he was quite friendly had turned away from him, not because they had anything against him but out of simple pragmatism: there was no point wasting their time with a journalist whose influence was clearly waning. His joy at being invited made him smile. He remembered how he used to groan at the excessive number of parties he was supposed to attend. In his decline, he was learning to love what he had formerly taken for granted.

Calmly drinking his beers, he had watched the ceaseless ballet of women coming and going from the lingerie shop. He'd imagined each customer undressing in the changing room, not in a lustful way, but more as a sort of innocent daydream. He thought it would surely be possible to understand the secrets and psychology of women by watching them buy underwear. This was one of his innumerable afternoon (alcohol) theories. When the last customer had left, Mathilde came out and locked up. It was then that she noticed the man who had questioned her hours earlier about her boss sitting in a bar on the other side of the street. Free of inhibitions by now, he gave her a big, friendly smile, as if they were old friends. The young woman was rather surprised by this striking transformation from the awkward, withdrawn person she had met before.

After smiling at her, Rouche waved in a way that might equally have suggested that he was wishing her a good evening or inviting her to join him. Mathilde could choose whichever option she preferred. Before we reveal her decision, however, one important fact must be explained: she didn't know anybody in Rennes. The higher the unemployment rate, the more easily people move away from home; and so, in times of economic crisis, it wasn't rare in cities to find entire crowds of lonely people. So she walked over to Rouche.

"You're still here?" she called out.

"Yes. I thought maybe she'd pop back this afternoon," he said, to justify his presence.

"Well, she didn't."

"Did she call you?"

"No."

"Would you like to have a drink with me?"

"…"

"Surely you can't say no to me three times in a row!"

"All right," said Mathilde with a smile.

The journalist stared at her in mild shock. It had been a long time since a strange woman had agreed to have a drink with him, spontaneously, without any professional obligation. He'd tried to be humorous, but he hadn't really expected it to work; so perhaps it was true that you were more likely to succeed when you had nothing to lose. He should pursue his investigation in that spirit. Just keep going, without thinking about the need for a result. But there was a consequence to this: she was there now, sitting next to him. So he was going to have to talk to her. Well yeah, he hadn't asked her to join him so they could share an awkward silence. But what should he say? What were the right words for this kind of situation? It didn't help matters that, from the moment when she agreed to have a drink with him, Rouche had started thinking how beautiful she was. This only increased his anxiety. It was too late: he had to be funny, interesting, charming. An impossible trio. Why the hell had he asked her to sit down? What an idiot! And how could she have agreed to have a drink with a man capable of scraping the same borrowed car twice in the same day? Yes, she had to take her share of blame for the present moment. While he thought all this, he masked his anguish with little fake smiles. But Rouche sensed that Mathilde could read all his emotions in his face. He had become incapable of pretending.

Thankfully, the waiter turned up just then. Mathilde ordered a beer, while Rouche asked for a Perrier, thinking that it was time to make a U-turn on the liquid road and head back towards sobriety. To avoid another embarrassing silence, he returned to the subject of his investigation.

"So you don't know where she is?"

"No, I told you."

"You're sure?"

"Are you a journalist or a cop?"

"I'm a journalist, don't worry."

"I'm not worried. Why, should I be?"

"No! No, not at all."

"Joséphine said she'd had enough of being interviewed. But it was very good for the shop."

Rouche didn't know what to say to this, so he just left a silence in the middle of their conversation. The tribulations he'd been through had robbed him of all social artifice. His face, too, had been transformed by his difficulties, changing cynicism to uncertainty, erasing the hard, severe frown lines to leave behind the face of a frightened boy, which inspired in others a blend of trust and pity. Mathilde, feeling exactly this combination of emotions, decided to tell him what she knew.

6

It had all begun about ten days earlier. Joséphine had come to the shop one morning looking very excited. A peculiar sight: she was standing completely still, yet you would have sworn that she was jumping for joy.

Mathilde, whose experience of her boss prior to this moment was of a woman who, although far from cold, was not the effusive type, was surprised to discover a new facet to her personality; Joséphine now seemed animated by an energy more typical of Mathilde's twenty-something friends. And, like any young person experiencing a feeling of exaltation, she could not keep it to herself. She felt compelled to tell all to the first person she encountered: her young salesgirl.

"It's incredible. I spent the night with Marc! Can you believe it? After so many years…"

Mathilde, unsure how seriously to take this declaration, opened her eyes wide. She had a certain talent for appearing enthusiastic. In fact, her reaction was primarily provoked by the astonishment of hearing such intimate confidences from the mouth of her boss, a woman she barely knew. She kept this same expression on her face as she listened to Joséphine go off on a long monologue.

So Marc was her ex-husband, who had suddenly left her for another woman. She'd found herself alone, since her two daughters had also left to open a restaurant in Berlin. With hindsight, that had perhaps been the hardest thing to bear: solitude. But it was her fault. She hadn't wanted to see friends, and particularly not any who had known her and Marc as a couple. Everything that reminded her of her lost marriage was painful. And in almost thirty years together, the memories had spread almost everywhere. In Rennes, she had to avoid all the neighbourhoods where they'd been out together, and that reduced the city to a tiny perimeter. Her despair was intensified by this prison-like geography.

But then he called her. When she answered, he said simply: "It's me." As if the legitimacy of that phrase was indestructible. In two words, he resurrected their intimacy. When two people have been together for a long time, they stop using each other's first names. After a few banal phrases about the passing of time, he admitted: "I saw you in the newspaper. It's crazy. I can't get over it. It did something to me."

"…"

"Incredible, that story about the novel your father wrote. I never would have believed it…"

"…"

166

"Hello? Are you there?"

Yes, she was there.

But, for the moment, she was incapable of speaking.

It was Marc, talking to her on the phone.

In the end he suggested they meet up.

She stammered her agreement.

7

Seeing each other again after several years, it felt like a first date. Joséphine was obsessed by her appearance: what would he think? She had aged, of course; she examined herself in the mirror for a long time, and was surprised to find that she looked beautiful. Yet she was not the type of woman to blow her own trumpet. On the contrary, she had often been guilty of endless, wearying bouts of self-deprecation. Recently, however, she had reconnected with the pleasures of life, and apparently that had rejuvenated her appearance. How could she have wasted so many years wallowing in misery? She felt almost ashamed at having suffered, as if the pain had not been something that happened to her but something she'd decided to feel. She had thought that it was all over, that she would now be able to bump into Marc in the street without pain, but she was wrong: hearing his voice on the phone, she realized immediately that she had never stopped loving him.

He arranged to meet her in a café where they used to eat lunch. Joséphine decided to get there early; she would rather be sitting down when he arrived. Above all, she didn't want to have to wander around the restaurant looking for him, with the risk of him observing her as she did so. She was annoyed at herself for fearing his opinion; she had nothing left to lose now.

Nothing had changed—the restaurant looked exactly the same—which added to her confusion. The past inhabited the present. She ordered a glass of red wine, after hesitating over a whole range of drink options, from herbal tea to apricot juice to champagne. Red wine struck her as a good compromise to mark the intensity of the moment without being overly celebratory. Everything seemed complicated to her; she even wondered how she should sit. Where should she position her arms, her hands, her legs, her gaze? Should she try to look more relaxed than she felt, or sit up very straight, as if on the lookout? He wasn't here yet, and she was already exhausted.

He finally arrived, a little early. He hurried over to her, smiling broadly.

"Ah, you're here already?"

"Yes, I had a meeting in the area…" Joséphine fibbed. They embraced warmly, then stood for a moment looking at each other and smiling.

At last, Marc said: "Strange, isn't it? Seeing each other again…"

"You must think I look horrible."

"Not at all! I saw you in the newspaper, you know. And I thought: she hasn't changed one bit. I'm the one who…"

"No, you're the same. Still as…"

"I've grown a belly," he interrupted.

He ordered red wine too, and they started talking, easily, fluently. It was as if they'd never been apart. Their complicity seemed absolute. Of course, they avoided the more difficult topics, for now. It's always simpler to get along if you talk about painless, neutral subjects, like recent films or trips or people who'd been mutual friends. They shared a few glasses over this light-hearted chatter. But was it real? Joséphine couldn't stop thinking about the other woman. The burning question was on her lips, as impossible to hold back as a man fleeing a house on fire.

"And what about her? Are you still together?"

"No. It's over. It's been several months now."

"Oh really? Why?"

"It was complicated. We weren't getting along…"

"Did she want children?" Joséphine guessed.

"Yes. But it wasn't just that. I didn't love her."

"How long did it take you to work that out?"

"Not long. But since I'd destroyed our marriage for her, I lied to myself. Right up until the moment when I decided to leave her."

"And why did you want to see me again?"

"I told you. I saw you in the newspaper. It was like a sign. I don't usually read the paper, as you know. To start with, I didn't feel like I had a right to call you. I put you through so much. And, well, I didn't know what your situation was…"

"I don't believe that. The girls must have told you."

"According to them, you're still single. But you might not tell them everything…"

"I don't hide anything from them. There hasn't been anyone since you. I could have… but I never could."

"…"

For the first time that evening, a silence deepened between them. Marc suggested they eat dinner somewhere else. Although she felt certain that she wouldn't be able to swallow a single morsel, she agreed.

8

During the meal, Joséphine had to acknowledge the strange destination to which this evening was headed. This was not like one of those normal reunions where you filled each other in about the years spent apart; no, it was something else altogether. Marc spoke more and more clearly about his desire to see her again. Besides, wasn't this what she had been dreaming of? He kept repeating how much he missed her, his desire for the past, the mistakes he had made. Sometimes, talking about his new hopes, he would lower his head. Marc was usually such a confident man, even a little arrogant, but here he was, groping around in the darkness. Seeing him in such disarray, Joséphine's feelings intensified, as did her self-assurance. She was more surprised than anyone by how at ease she felt, but it was true; in that moment, everything was clear. She had lived through the last few years waiting only for this instant. She used her napkin to wipe a drop of sweat from her ex-husband's forehead, and that was how it all began again.

A little later, they made love at Marc's apartment. It was a peculiar feeling, being reunited with such a familiar body after so many years. Joséphine felt a first-timer's fear mingled with a perfect knowledge of her lover. But one thing had changed: Marc's determination to give her pleasure. She'd always enjoyed sex with him, but it had become mechanical in their later years. His erotic attentions had become very rare. That night, the opposite was true. Her husband was charged with a new energy. Through his body, he wished to give her proof that he had changed. Joséphine wanted to abandon herself to the pleasure, but she couldn't free herself from consciousness of the act. It would take her more time to be able to make love without thinking about it. Nevertheless, the pleasure she felt was real, and the two of them remained stunned by what had happened. Joséphine ended up falling asleep in Marc's arms. When she opened her eyes, she realized that everything she had experienced was real.

9

During the days that followed, they continued along this path. They met in the evenings to eat dinner, talked about memories and mistakes, hopes and plans, and ended the night making love at Marc's apartment. He seemed happy and fulfilled; little by little, he told Joséphine how the other woman had suffocated him, depriving him of the space he needed, attempting to control his life. She'd needed to be reassured with gifts, money. Joséphine did not enjoy hearing all this. It sent her back into the pain she'd felt and, ultimately, left a bitter taste in her mouth. They had to move beyond the past.

"Please don't talk about it any more…"

"Yes, you're right. I'm sorry."

"It's over."

Suddenly changing the subject, Marc asked: "Could you ever have imagined your father was capable of writing a story like that?"

"What?"

"Your father's book… Could you have imagined it?"

"No. But then I couldn't have predicted what's happened with us either. So anything is possible."

"Yes, you're right. But we don't sell so many books!"

"True."

"Do you know the figures?"

"Of what?"

"Well… your father's sales. I read in the papers that his book has sold more than 300,000 copies."

"Yes, I think so. And it's still selling."

"That's huge," said Marc.

"I'm not sure I realize what it means, really. But yes, I think it's a lot."

"Believe me, it really is."

"It's just strange, more than anything. My parents worked their whole lives, they never had much money, and suddenly my father leaves behind a book that will make my mother rich. You know her, though. She couldn't care less about money. It wouldn't surprise me if she gave it all to charity."

"You think? That'd be a shame. You should talk to her about it. You could make all your dreams come true. Buy yourself a boat at last…"

"Ah, you remember…"

"Of course. I remember everything. Everything."

Joséphine was surprised that he should recall that particular detail. The desire for a boat was something that went back to her childhood. For Joséphine, true freedom was possible only on the water. She had grown up close to the Atlantic and spent her childhood looking out to sea. When she returned to Crozon, it was often the first thing she did, even before going to see her mother: say hello to the ocean. She fell asleep thinking about that boat, which she might be able to buy. Until now, she hadn't asked her mother about the royalties that the book was earning. Their life was bound to change.

I O

For now, the consequences were mostly media-related. Joséphine continued to receive calls from journalists asking her for interviews and new details. She promised she would do some research, but she couldn't really think of anything that would be useful. They hadn't given up. Letters? Official documents? Something had flashed in her memory then: she felt almost certain that her father had written her a letter during the summer she turned nine. She'd received it when she was at a holiday camp in the south of France. She remembered it, because it was the only one. Back then, nobody used the phone to keep in touch during separations. So her father must have decided to write to her. What had she done with that letter? What did it say? She had to find it, come what may. It would finally be a written trace left behind by her father. The more she thought about it, the more firmly she believed that he had deliberately not left any such writings behind. A man capable of writing such a great novel in secrecy knew exactly what he was doing.

Where could she have put it? Even while she slept, Joséphine couldn't stop thinking about it. That night in her dreams, she drew close to the place where she'd left the letter. It took her a couple more nights to find the solution. People who don't sleep deeply are either exhausted or exhausting for others. Joséphine lived constantly in the middle of this bipolar rhythm, her days alternating between a sort of slow-motion life and a life surging with energy. Every morning, in the shop, Mathilde waited to see if she would be working with a mollusc or a dynamo. Recently, the dynamo had prevailed. Joséphine talked nonstop. She felt a need to tell everybody she saw about what she was experiencing, and as the person she saw most often was Mathilde, she bore the brunt of these monologues. The young salesgirl listened—with a certain pleasure, it must be said—to the details of Marc and Joséphine's reunion. It was enjoyable to see this woman, whom she genuinely liked (she had hired her, after all) gesticulating like somebody thirty years younger.

The next night, Joséphine dived even deeper into her memories, attempting to retrieve the letter's hiding place. After her divorce, she had dumped a load of cardboard boxes in Crozon, but she remembered keeping her collection of records. She had thought about getting rid of them, as she no longer had a turntable on which to play them, but those vinyl discs reminded her strongly of her adolescence. All she had to do was look at one of the record sleeves and a memory would instantly bubble up. In her dream, she saw herself slipping her father's letter inside one of those record sleeves; she had done this more than thirty years before, thinking to herself: "One day, I will listen to this album and I'll be surprised to find the letter." Yes, she felt certain that this was what she'd done. But which album was it? She told Mathilde that she had to go home to listen to some old records. The salesgirl did not appear surprised, as if the past few days had accustomed her to her boss's strange behaviour.

I I

As she drove towards her apartment, Joséphine thought about The Beatles and Pink Floyd, about Bob Dylan and Alain

Souchon, about Janis Joplin and Michel Berger, and so many others. Why didn't she listen to that music any more? In the shop, she would sometimes put Radio Nostalgie on in the background, but without really listening to it. She remembered how feverishly excited she had felt every time she'd bought a new album, how eager she'd been to listen to it. When she listened to a record, that was all she did; sitting on her bed, looking at the sleeve, letting the music fill her soul. But all that was over. She'd got married, had two daughters, and stopped listening to her albums. And then CDs had arrived, the new technology giving her an excuse for her vinyl neglect.

When she got home, she went down to the cellar to collect the two dusty cardboard boxes. Of course, she felt excited, in a hurry to find the letter, but looking at those old record sleeves gave her so much pleasure that she ended up taking her time. Each album was a memory, a moment, an emotion. Looking through them, she found herself face-to-face with scenes from her life, dark melancholy moods mixed with uncontrollable laughter. She looked inside each one, hoping that the letter would fall out. She used to enjoy slipping little notes, cinema tickets and other papers into those album sleeves, hiding these ephemeral scraps inside her music so that they would return to her sooner or later. Her life came back to her, bit by bit; all the Joséphines of the past joined her in this nostalgic reunion, and it was here, surrounded by her past, that she found her father's letter.

It was hidden in an album by Barbara, *Le Mal de Vivre*. Why had she put her father's letter in that particular record sleeve? Instead of opening the letter, as she ought to have done, she spent a moment contemplating the record. This was the album that featured the beautiful track, "Göttingen". Joséphine remembered listening obsessively to that song; she'd been a huge fan of the singer at the time. The passion had been a fleeting one, as so many adolescent passions are, but she'd spent several months entranced by Barbara's dark, melancholy melodies. She downloaded "Göttingen" to her phone so she could listen to it again now, and immediately fell under the spell of those words:

> Of course, we have the Seine
> And our Bois de Vincennes,
> But how beautiful the roses are
> In Göttingen, in Göttingen.

> We have our pale mornings
> And Verlaine's grey soul,
> But true melancholy lives
> In Göttingen, in Göttingen.

Barbara was paying a sublime tribute to that city, and in particular to the German people. In 1964, this was a brave act. As a Jewish child who had spent the war in hiding, the singer had hesitated for a long time before performing in what had once been enemy territory. When she first went there, her attitude was far from friendly. She had a tantrum about the piano, and finally appeared on stage two hours late. It made no difference: she was cheered, adored. The organizers did everything they could to make her visit a success. She had never received such a welcome anywhere before, and she was moved to tears by it. She decided to extend her stay, and wrote those few lines, which are more powerful than any speech. Joséphine didn't know the whole story behind this song, but she was overwhelmed by the melody, like a carousel that takes you in its arms. Perhaps that was why she'd put her father's letter in this cover. With Barbara's song playing in the background, she reread the words he had written forty years before. Her father returned from beyond the grave to whisper them in her ear.

When she got back to the shop, Joséphine decided to put the letter in the small safe where she usually kept her cash. The afternoon was frantic, with far more customers than usual; there was something strangely intense about this whole day. The past few weeks, in fact, had marked a break from the previous years, as if her life was avenging itself for the emptiness, the absence of human adventures.

That evening, Marc came to pick Joséphine up outside the shop. Mathilde discreetly observed this man, whom her boss talked about constantly. He was not at all how she'd imagined him. There was a total disconnect between the Marc that had formed in her head during all of Joséphine's anecdotes, and the real Marc who stood on the pavement smoking a cigarette. She instinctively preferred the imaginary one, the one she'd invented based on Joséphine's words.

After dinner, they went back to Marc's place. Joséphine preferred it that way. She wasn't at ease with the idea of inviting
him to hers, as if her apartment would give him too many clues
about her. She had told Marc about the letter she'd found.
She was happy to share that moment with him; he seemed
enthusiastic, and kept repeating how amazing the whole story
was. Then he added:

"Like our reunion…"

"Yes."

"Do you like Richard Burton?" Marc asked, for no apparent reason.

"Who?"

"Richard Burton, the actor."

"Oh yeah, the one who was in *Cleopatra*. Liz Taylor's husband. Why are you asking me about him?"

"Well, you know they got married, then divorced, and then
they got married again…"

"…"

What was he trying to say? Was this a proposal? Since
they'd started sleeping together again, she had promised herself not to imagine anything. Just to let herself be guided by
this unexpected pleasure. Marc eventually observed: "You're
not saying anything."

"…", agreed Joséphine.

Marc took Joséphine by the hand to lead her towards the bed,
but she preferred to remain on the sofa. She was paralysed by

her feelings. Suddenly she started crying. The beauty of tears is that they can have two completely different meanings. You cry with pain, and you cry with happiness. Very few physical acts have such a Janus-like duality, as if to manifest confusion. But in that instant, Joséphine's hand brushed a scrap of fabric under the sofa cushion. She looked down and saw a pair of lacy knickers.

"What's that?"

"I don't know," Marc said, embarrassed. He grabbed the underwear.

Joséphine listened to him stammer his explanation. He didn't understand how the underwear had ended up here. It must have fallen into the sofa, and slipped back out when they sat down. It was absurd; better just to laugh about it.

"Are you still seeing her?" Joséphine asked.

"No. Of course not."

"Why did you lie?"

"I didn't! I'm telling you the truth."

"Why should I believe you?"

"I swear! I haven't seen her in a long time. Our break-up was acrimonious. She lived here a long time, though, so it's possible that her knickers have been here the whole time, hidden inside the sofa."

"..."

"Please don't make a big deal out of this."

Marc pronounced those words with real conviction. All the same, Joséphine felt bitter. This apparition of a ghost from the past, particularly in the form of lingerie, just as they were

talking about getting married again… Was it a sign? Marc
kept talking, attempting to downplay the incident. He threw
the knickers out of the window, ridding himself of them in
a theatrical, amusing way. Joséphine agreed to forget it and
move on. Still, there was no more talk about marriage that
evening.

13

That night, she couldn't fall asleep. The little scrap of silk
discovered under a cushion kept her awake; she couldn't stop
thinking about it. Marc slept next to her, alternating—as was
his habit—between periods of snoring and periods of silence
(a double life, even in his sleep?). Beside him, on the bedside
table, was his mobile; Joséphine started obsessing over the idea
of turning it on and reading his messages. She had never gone
through his things when they were married, not even when
she'd had good reason to be suspicious; it was not necessarily
a question of trust, but of respect for the other's freedom. But,
in the middle of this night, it seemed to her that things were
different. She was fifty; too old to make a wrong choice. He
wanted to remarry her; she couldn't walk into it like this, eyes
closed and heart open.

Silently she got out of bed and picked up the phone. Then
she locked herself in the bathroom. What an idiot! Of course
the phone had a security code. She tried one that didn't
work. Obviously he hadn't chosen their anniversary date.

She had two more attempts left. It was absurd, trying to read his messages; she knew him better than anyone. They'd lived together for nearly thirty years, they had two daughters: what could she hope to find? She knew his qualities, his flaws, and sometimes the two were connected. She'd read in an article that more and more couples were getting back together. It was no longer rare to reunite with your first love, and to live together a second time, armed with your knowledge of each other. She couldn't be disappointed by Marc any more; she'd been too disappointed in the past. Even though she reasoned to herself in this way, she couldn't help continuing to think about what his code might be. Marc adored his daughters, and often went to see them in Berlin. Perhaps he'd simply used their two birth dates—the 15th and the 18th—side by side.

She tried "1518" and the phone unlocked.

Joséphine gaped. Never had she thought she would guess the code so easily. She had been driven by an urge that had been doomed, in all probability, to remain unfulfilled. And yet, fate had decided otherwise. It felt almost like divine intervention. On the other side of the door she could still hear Marc's heavy breathing. She clicked on "Messages" and saw Pauline's name appear—the name that she had always refused to utter, the name for which she had developed an inordinate hatred, without knowing whether it was deserved or not. So the first thing to note was: Marc was lying. He *was* still in contact with her. And the most recent message was dated today—that very evening.

Sitting on the bathroom floor, Joséphine felt nauseous. Did she need to go any further? Her nausea faded, leaving behind a cold anger. She read all the messages—and there were so many. Messages of love, promises to see each other soon, discussions of the plan, which was working perfectly. The plan was her. But what plan? Why? She didn't understand. It was enough to drive her insane. Her breathing became erratic and uncontrollable, her body was in open revolt; she could no longer contain the fire that was spreading inside her.

At that moment, Marc knocked at the door:

"Are you there, my love?"

"…"

"What are you doing?"

"…"

"Are you okay? I'm worried. Open the door."

Marc heard Joséphine's breathing, which sounded like she was suffocating. What was happening? Perhaps she was having a seizure…

"If you don't open the door, I'll call an ambulance."

"No," she said coldly.

"But what's going on?"

"…"

Joséphine was still staring at the screen of the phone, reading messages that talked of money. Suddenly, everything was clear. Trembling, she no longer heard Marc's pleas. He begged her to open the door, to reply, to explain herself. What should she do? Open the door and slap him as hard as she could? Or leave without saying a word? She felt so sick, she didn't feel capable of a confrontation. She stood up, splashed some water on her face. In the end, she left the bathroom and headed towards the sofa, where she'd left her belongings.

"What's happening? I was so worried!"

"…"

"What are you doing? Why are you getting dressed?"

"…"

"I know you don't want to answer. But please, tell me!"

"Look in the bathroom, and leave me alone," Joséphine said.

Marc went in and immediately saw his mobile on the tile floor. He turned to Joséphine and begged her: "I'm so sorry. Please forgive me. I'm so ashamed…"

"…"

"I've been wanting to talk to you about this for a few days now. Really, I have. Because everything was so wonderful with you, and I felt so good."

"Shut up. That's all I ask of you: just shut your mouth. I'm going, and I never want to see you again."

Suddenly Marc took Joséphine in his arms and pleaded with her. She shoved him away violently. Infuriated, she demanded: "But why? Why did you do this to me? How could you?"

"I had problems. Serious problems. I have no money left at all. I lost it all… and I realized that you were going to be rich…"

"You wanted to marry me, take my money… and then go back to your whore? Do you realize what you're saying?"

"I wasn't rational. I'd lost it completely. But yes, I realize. I… I'm pathetic."

"I can't believe how much pain you've put me through."

"…"

Marc started weeping; this was the first time Joséphine had ever seen him in tears. No tragedy had ever done this to him before. But it changed nothing. She left without a word. Let him rot in his mediocrity. Outside, she tried to find a cab, in vain. She wandered through the night for nearly an hour.

Joséphine had spent years putting herself back together, and, barely had she started to recover than Marc killed her again. And all this because of that cursed novel. When he was alive, her father had hardly ever hugged her, and now he'd left behind a book that was wreaking devastation. She had suffered through all those years, but that wasn't enough. She had to suffer even more; she had to live through the last hours of a love affair, as if her death throes were not over yet.

14

The next morning, she waited for Mathilde to arrive at the shop, before telling her that she was going to be away *for a while*.

15

Rouche had listened to Mathilde's account with intense concentration, hoping to come across some small detail that might prove crucial for his investigation. Of course, all he'd heard was what the salesgirl knew: a partial version of the drama that had played out in Joséphine's life. But, amid the turmoil of recent events, one fact stuck out: the letter written by Pick. Rouche decided not to ask about this straight away (he would wait until his second question):

"And have you heard from her since then?"

"No, not a word. I tried to call, but I just got her voice-mail."

"And the letter?"

"What letter?"

"The letter from her father. Did she take it with her?"

"No, it's still in the safe."

Mathilde pronounced these words without understanding their importance for Jean-Michel. He was so close to a written trace of Pick.[19] Mathilde observed him, amused.

"Are you okay?" she asked.

"Yeah, I'm fine. I think I'll order another beer. Perrier is depressing."

Mathilde smiled. She liked the company of this strange-looking older man; she'd found him somewhat repellent to start with, but after spending time with him she could detect a certain charm (or was it the alcohol?). She felt increasingly moved by him, by the way he always seemed so surprised, like a man who couldn't quite believe he was

19 Like Christopher Columbus, one foot suspended above the earth of the American continent.

still alive. He had the special energy of a survivor: he was satisfied with so little.

As for Rouche, he didn't dare look Mathilde in the eyes, preferring to stare at the lamp post in front of him, a lamp post that he could have described more easily than he could the salesgirl's face. He was beginning to find it a little odd that she was giving him so much of her time. And yet she had admitted that she didn't know anybody in this city. That's what it takes for a girl to spend an hour with me, he thought. Before, he could talk, charmingly, wittily, without any problem at all; now, each word he uttered was first weighed up, examined, before being stammered. His professional fall from grace had stolen his self-confidence. Thankfully, he'd met Brigitte, and he loved her; or at any rate, he thought he still loved her. She was the one who seemed to be distancing herself from him. They rarely made love any more, and he missed it. By some strange mechanism, the more Jean-Michel talked with Mathilde, the closer he felt to Brigitte. This did not prevent him feeling desire for this young woman, but his heart remained under the consoling thumb of the owner of a twice-scratched car.

Just before midnight, Rouche finally dared ask Mathilde to go and get the letter.

"I should ask Joséphine first, don't you think?"

"Please. Just show it to me."

"You're asking me to do a bad thing," she added, before bursting into laughter. It was a crucial moment; and, crucially, it was a moment when she had a considerable amount of alcohol in her bloodstream. "Okay, I'll do it, Mr Rouche," she said eventually. "Okay... but if I get into trouble over this, I'll tell them that you forced me to do it."

"Yes, all right. Like a hold-up."

"Or a bra-up!"

"Um... that doesn't mean anything."

"Yeah, that's true," Mathilde concluded, getting to her feet.

The journalist watched her go, amazed by her precise, gracious gait despite her long working day and all those beers. She returned two minutes later, the letter in her hands. Rouche took it from her and carefully opened it. He read it, then read it again. Several times. Then he looked up. Everything was clear now.

16

Mathilde watched in silence as the journalist seemed lost in thought. She didn't want to break his concentration. The coolness of the night was clearing her head. After a while she said: "So?"

"..."

"What do you think of it?"

"..."

"You don't have anything to tell me?"

"Thank you. Sincerely. Thank you."

"You're welcome."

"Can I keep it?" Rouche asked.

"No. You're asking too much now. I can't do that. That letter is important to her, I could tell."

"Let me make a copy, then. There must be a photocopier in the shop?"

"God, it never ends with you!"

"That's not something I hear very often," he replied with a smile.

They were calling each other *tu* instead of *vous* now (after how many beers had they started doing that?), and there was a genuine complicity between them. Would that have happened if they'd been drinking water? Probably. Anyway, they paid for their drinks then walked to the shop. At midnight, in the darkness, Rouche was frightened by the mannequins. He had the impression that they'd been talking to one another, just before he and Mathilde arrived. They froze in the presence of humans, but the rest of the time they talked about their escape plans. Why was he thinking such nonsense at a moment like this? Mathilde photocopied the letter and handed him the copy.

17

Outside on the street, Rouche finally gave some thought to practical matters. He had not booked a hotel room. He asked Mathilde if she knew a good place nearby. "Not too expensive," he specified.

"You can sleep at my place, if you want…"

Rouche didn't know how to respond. What did this mean exactly? In the end, he decided to drive her home, to give him time to think. When they arrived at her apartment, he said: "You shouldn't invite strangers to sleep at your place like that."

"You're hardly a stranger."

"I could be a psychopath. After all, I was a literary critic for several years."

"Well, maybe you should be wary too. What makes you so sure that I'm not a serial killer of depressive old men?"

"True."

They continued to talk playfully like this for a while as they sat in the car. As often happens after a night of drinking, it was becoming difficult to distinguish seduction from simple camaraderie. What did Mathilde want? Perhaps she was simply tired of being alone. In the end, Rouche decided not to go upstairs. This was not necessarily a triumph of mind over body, but it was a reasonable choice, and he was happy to have made it. For several minutes, he had been thinking semi-constantly about Brigitte. His conclusion was that things were not over between them. Despite some recent difficulties, he did not want to admit defeat. He loved her, perhaps even more right now. Of course, he could have gone to Mathilde's room, and maybe nothing would have happened; in fact, that was quite likely. But he wouldn't have been able to sleep, knowing that she was close by. No, it was better to stay in the car. He'd sleep on the back seat, with the photocopy of Pick's letter. After all, his mission was what mattered; he should stay focused on that.

18

They embraced for a long moment. Then Mathilde went to her apartment and Jean-Michel thought he would never see her again.

19

To begin with, nothing had struck Hervé Maroutou as abnormal. He just felt a bit more tired than he had in previous days; but he was getting older, after all, and being a sales representative was not exactly a restful occupation. Not to mention the increasing pressure. With the ever-growing numbers of books being published, he had to fight ever harder for the ones he represented to be displayed prominently on bookshop shelves. Or, even better, in bookshop windows. As a connoisseur of the region, and having patiently formed relationships with the booksellers here, Maroutou was held in esteem by everybody who knew him. He still felt the same shiver of pleasure at reading a novel before the rest of the world, at receiving it long before publication so that he could present it to his customers. Highly motivated by that meeting at Grasset, he had managed to communicate the publishers' enthusiasm for Pick's book. And look at the results! The novel was going from strength to strength. Hervé had just received an invitation to a party to celebrate that success; this made him happy. It was normal for sales reps to be pampered at the start of the bookselling process, but after a book had become a success they were rarely included in the festivities. That oversight had been fixed with this party, which he envisaged as the grand finale to an extraordinary literary adventure.

After a few weeks, he had to face the reality: this was no ordinary fatigue. One morning, he got out of bed and vomited, and had a terrible headache for the rest of the day. His lower back hurt too: a strange, burning pain. For the first time in a long time, he cancelled all his meetings, because he felt incapable of driving or speaking. He was staying at the Mercure hotel in Nancy at the time. He decided to consult a doctor. He had to call several numbers before he found someone who would see him. In the waiting room, he felt too sick to look through the old magazines scattered across the table. The only thing he cared about was putting an end to his pain. Even though he hadn't eaten anything that morning, he again felt like he was going to vomit. He trembled, but felt hot. It was as if his body was a theatre of war between two armies. Little by little, he lost all sense of time. How long had he been waiting there?

Finally, his name was called. The doctor had a yellowish complexion; he looked sickly. Who wants to be healed by a dying man? The doctor asked him several questions in a mechanical manner. The usual interrogation about the patient's family history. Maroutou felt reassured: the doctor was listening to him, he would find whatever was wrong with him. After a few pills and some rest, he'd be back at work. The first place he would go was a bookshop called the Hall du Livre, because he liked the owner; she had shown great confidence in him by ordering a hundred copies of Pick's book.

"Cough, please," said the doctor.

"I can't," he replied. "I don't feel well."

"Yes, your breathing is laboured."

"What do you think it is?"

"You'll need to do some more advanced tests."

"Can I do that in a few days?" asked Maroutou. "When I get back to Paris?"

"Um… The sooner the better," said the doctor, sounding apprehensive.

A few hours later, at the hospital in Nancy, Maroutou was standing bare-chested against a cold imaging plate. This was the first in a series of tests. Not a good sign. The doctors kept wanting to *refine the diagnosis*. When you're fine, they always know straight away. Refining the diagnosis meant something was definitely wrong, they just weren't sure exactly what. There was no point beating about the bush; he could tell it was bad news from the expressions on the doctors' faces. In the end, one of them asked Hervé if he wanted to know the truth. What was he supposed to say? "No, I took all those tests, but don't tell me anything." Of course he wanted to know. It was the doctor who seemed reluctant to speak. Then again, you probably don't become a doctor for the pleasure of telling someone that they're going to die.

"When?" Hervé asked.

"Soon…"

What did that mean, *soon*? One day, one week, one year?

According to the doctor, *soon* could mean a few months. In the end, though, what did that change? The news marked the end of his life. He thought about his wife a bit more than usual. She had died of cancer at thirty-four, when they were trying to have a child. None of his colleagues knew this. Hervé Maroutou had lived the nomadic life of a sales rep because he had sworn never to become involved with anyone else. Twenty years later, he found himself in an echo of the same sad scene. With one major difference: he was alone with his fear. He had at least been able to hold his wife's hand when she found out, and they had loved each other until her last breath. He had never forgotten the last hours of their love, hours that were, paradoxically, peaceful and serene. All that remained was the essential: the absolute, crazy love of a man accompanying his wife to her death. Was she waiting for him on the other side? No, he didn't believe that. Her body had decomposed a long time ago, and his would soon follow suit.

20

On the day of the party organized by Grasset, Maroutou summoned enough strength to attend; it would do him good, surely, to see some of his friends and colleagues. He had to force himself to live. Who knows? Maybe he could drive the disease back, as other people had done. But he didn't have the necessary energy to fight it; alone, he let himself drift towards his final day, hoping only that he wouldn't suffer too much.

He felt exhausted, so he ordered a whisky at the bar then went to sit at the back of the room, away from the crowds. The party already resembled the end of a wedding; it was only eight o'clock, yet everybody looked drunk. Sitting in his corner, Maroutou was joined by a grey-haired man.

"Good evening. May I sit with you?"

"Sure," Maroutou replied.

"Rouche," the man introduced himself.

"Ah, I didn't recognize you. I remember your articles."

"Would you like me to sit somewhere else?"

"No, not at all. Maroutou. Hervé Maroutou. Pleased to meet you."

"Pleased to meet you too."

The two men shook hands. Each man's grip was so limp that their handshake was about as energetic as a neurasthenic mollusc.

They made some small talk about their only visible point in common: they were both drinking whisky.

"So what do you do?" asked Rouche.

"I work for Grasset. I'm a rep. Based in the east of France."

"That must be interesting."

"I won't be doing it for much longer."

"Ah? You're retiring?"

"No, I'm going to die."

"…"

Rouche went pale, then stammered his condolences.

"I'm sorry," Hervé said. "I don't know why I said that to you. Nobody else knows. I don't talk about it normally. And then, suddenly, out it comes. Tough luck for you."

"Don't apologize. It probably had to come out. I'm there for you, if you… well, I mean, I'm probably not the most joyful company…"

"Why?"

"No, it's ridiculous. You've just told me you're dying, so I'm not going to bother you with my small problems."

"Please do," Maroutou insisted.

It was a bizarre situation, thought Rouche; he was going to complain about his misfortunes in order to entertain a dying man. In the past few days, his life had taken a strange turn; he felt like a character in a novel.

"It's my wife," began Rouche, then he immediately fell silent.

"What about your wife?"

"Well, she's not actually my wife. We're not married."

"Go on…"

"She just left me."

"Ah, I'm sorry. How long were you together?"

"Three years. And it hadn't been going well, but I do think I loved her. Well, maybe not. I don't know. I clung to her, to our relationship, because my life was a mess."

"If it's not too indiscreet, why did she decide to leave you?"

"Because of her car."

2 1

This was a somewhat crude summary of the situation, but not entirely false. After sleeping in the Volvo, Rouche had decided to drive back to Paris. The letter he'd acquired was all he needed for his investigation, for now at least. It was a crucial piece of evidence. Thinking back to his evening with Mathilde, he felt happy. You have to be wary of moments like that, he thought afterwards, as if admitting that his happiness rendered him suddenly fragile.

When he got home, he rested for most of the afternoon, then took a shower before Brigitte's arrival. When she turned up, he immediately tried to tell her about his discovery, but she seemed uninterested. He felt bitter about this. Rouche had dreamt that the story might bring them together again, that it would be a source of complicity, a subject that would lead to lively discussions. Now he was alone with the dead author he planned to unmask. Instead, she interrogated him:

"Did everything go okay with the car?"

"…"

"Why aren't you saying anything?"

"Um, no reason."

"What happened?"

"Nothing. Well, almost nothing."

"Where are you parked?"

He followed her downstairs, like a man walking towards his own execution. Brigitte looked horrified when she saw the car. Jean-Michel argued that it wasn't too bad, that it would be easy to fix. In other circumstances, the incident might not have seemed so important, but given the increasingly ominous atmosphere between them, she saw it as symbolic. She'd decided to trust him, and this was the result. Brigitte stared at the two scratches, as if the car's bodywork represented her own heart. Suddenly she felt exhausted at not being loved the way she wanted to be.

"I think we should separate."

"What? You're not going to leave me for a scratch?"

"There are two."

"Does it matter? We're not going to split up over that."

"I'm leaving you because I don't love you any more."

"If I'd taken the train, would we still be together?"

"..."

After spending the previous evening with Mathilde, Rouche had realized that he still loved Brigitte; but it was too late. He'd disappointed her too many times. These were their last hours as a couple. Jean-Michel clung to the illusion that everything would work itself out, but the look in Brigitte's eyes left no room for doubt. There was no point pleading for a reprieve. It was over. He felt an intense burning pain in his body, which surprised him. He thought he'd been bled dry by his trials and tribulations; he had no idea that his heart was still capable of aching.

22

After listening to Rouche's account, Maroutou agreed that it was difficult to accept as a reason for ending a relationship. But the journalist made excuses for Brigitte, remembering that she had probably saved his life at a time when he was close to going under. In the end, he couldn't blame her. The two men drank another whisky to this, before continuing their conversation about Pick.

"So you've investigated that story?" Maroutou asked.

"Yes."

"You don't think he's the author?"

"I know he's not," said Rouche, lowering his voice, as if what he'd just revealed was an affair of state likely to imperil the world's geopolitical equilibrium.

The louder and more raucous the party grew, the more the two men slumped into their chairs. There is a moment when the joy of others accentuates your own distress. A woman walked past them and said: "You two remind me of Woody Allen and Martin Landau at the end of *Crimes and Misdemeanors*."

"Ah, thank you," said Rouche, uncertain whether it was a compliment. He didn't remember that film. Maroutou hadn't seen it; he had always preferred reading books to going to the cinema. But did it really matter any more, what he liked? All the books he'd read and championed now formed a heap of incomprehensible words; it seemed to him that nothing of beauty remained to him. And he saw his own life as grotesque.

"I'm going to get us a couple more whiskies," said Rouche.

"Good idea," said his companion, although he could barely hear his own voice. Maroutou felt chaotic vibrations: a humming that made it impossible for him to distinguish anything beyond his own thoughts. The CEO of Éditions Grasset, Olivier Nora, was giving a short speech thanking everybody for their hard work; he singled out Delphine Despero. Maroutou recognized the young editor, who seemed a little overwhelmed at being the centre of attention. For the first time, she looked as if she were losing her self-assurance. It made her seem more human, more likeable. Her boss asked her to say a few words. Even though she must have prepared her speech in advance, she tripped over her words a little bit. Everybody was staring at her, including her loved ones. Her parents were there, and Frédéric too, of course, smiling broadly. The only person missing was a representative of the author's family; Joséphine had been invited, but she hadn't come. They had tried in vain to contact her.

From his seat at the back of the room, and despite his somewhat blurred vision, Maroutou saw all of this. He thought Delphine looked like a teenager lost in the oversized suit of a grown-up. Suddenly he stood up and walked nervously towards her. He didn't hear Rouche asking him where he was going. A few people turned to look at this man, who strode ostentatiously through the crowd; this man who brusquely took the microphone from Delphine and uttered the following words: "All right, that's enough now! Everybody knows that Pick didn't write that book!"

PART EIGHT

I

T HE NEWS WAS in the next day's papers, and social media went wild over it. Conspiracy theorists had a field day. There is such a great temptation nowadays not to believe the official version of anything. The head of Grasset was of the opinion that a small controversy might actually boost the book's sales, while categorically rejecting the hypothesis that *The Last Hours of a Love Affair* was written by another author. The novelist Frédéric Beigbeder jumped on the bandwagon to write an article unmasking himself as Pick. After all, the novel had been published by his publisher. And, as a Russian expert (one of his novels was set there), he obviously knew all about Pushkin. It was perfectly plausible. For a few days, the press pack pursued him, and he took advantage of this to announce to all and sundry the details of his new novel. In marketing terms, it was a huge coup. Now the title of his novel, *Friendship (Also) Lasts Three Years*, was on everyone's lips.

Of course, Beigbeder did not write Pick's novel. And in fact there was nothing to prove what Maroutou had so vehemently declared in the middle of that party. The rumour was that the sales rep had been completely drunk that night, and that he'd been egged on by the journalist Jean-Michel Rouche. So it was that the feeding frenzy turned to Rouche. It was said that he knew the truth about this story. Rouche refused to explain the reasons for his conviction. How ironic it was to be the centre of public attention after having been the most scorned leper in Paris! All those people who'd been ignoring his phone calls were suddenly desperate to see him again. But his initial pleasure at this turnaround soon turned to disgust for the entire farce. He decided not to say anything at all. He was in possession of Pick's letter, probably the only one that the dead pizzeria owner ever wrote; he was not going to gift it to the mob.

It was not only a question of vengeance: although he felt certain, he didn't want to reveal anything until he was in a position to reveal everything. This was his story, and he would have to be discreet now if he wanted the opportunity to follow it to its conclusion. Maroutou's impromptu speech had complicated matters. Rouche had the glimmer of an idea about the identity of the author who had hidden behind Pick's name, but he wasn't about to confide it to anyone, not even another alcoholic who would soon be dead. The only person he might have told was Brigitte. But she was no longer there to listen to him. Since their separation, she had refused to answer his calls. He'd left a wide variety of messages on her voicemail, in every tone from humour to despair, but they all fell on deaf ears. When he walked the streets, he constantly looked out for Volvos; after Pick, they were his main obsession. Whenever he saw one, he would quickly check its bodywork. Not one of them had a scratch on it. From this, he concluded that everybody was loved except for him.

2

This time, Rouche took the train. He'd always liked this form of transport, because it allowed him to read. Why hadn't he gone by train last time? You could lose yourself in your thoughts without risking damage to the vehicle. For him, it was an opportunity to get a little further through Bolaño's novel. It was such a unique experience. As a big fan of German literature, Rouche was fascinated by the feverish narration of *2666*, and the intermingling of several books within one giant project. Stories lost themselves within narrative labyrinths. In his head, he created two teams: García Márquez, Borges and Bolaño against Kafka, Mann and Musil. Between them, a man who had wavered between these two worlds, whom he mentally designated the referee: Gombrowicz. The journalist slipped into a pleasant daydream of this literary battle, rewriting the history of a century through commas.

Suddenly, it all made sense: he was going to a library.

Why had he never written a novel? In truth, he had tried, several times. Pages and pages of sterile attempts. And then he had started judging the work of others, often quite severely. That had made it seem impossible for him to publish a novel, even one as mediocre as those he read. Leafing through certain books, though, he would still think to himself: why not me? By the end of this long path, a mix of envy and frustration, Rouche had definitively abandoned the idea. It was almost a relief, admitting to himself that he did not possess the ability to write. He'd lived in this oppressive atmosphere of unfulfilled promise, with the feeling of not having accomplished what he might have done. Perhaps that was why the library of rejected books had struck such a chord with him. He understood perfectly the act of renunciation.

3

In Crozon, that day, the rain poured down. It was impossible to see anything; he might have been anywhere.

4

As he didn't have enough money to take a taxi, Rouche had to wait in the station for the rain to stop. Sitting close to the sandwich shop, he attracted quite a bit of attention. Some passers-by took him for a beggar, although he himself didn't realize this. It was mostly because of his raincoat, which was threadbare in places. Rouche had always felt good in that coat, which made him look like an unfinished novel. He could have bought a new one; Brigitte had suggested that they go shopping[20] for one on several occasions. She would tell him that there was a sale, but it made no difference; he preferred to live and die in the same old, ratty coat.

20 Probably Rouche's most hated activity, along with the practice of any kind of sport; he was driven crazy by the mere idea of entering a Zara or an H&M, above all because of the music.

Brigitte had left him now, but his coat was still with him. This thought struck him as incongruous. How many women had he been through since he first bought this raincoat? He remembered every moment, and could reconstruct a large part of his romantic life through the prism of its worn fabric. He saw again the moments spent with Justine, his raincoat clinging to the coat rack of a chic brasserie in Paris; the trip to Ireland with Isabelle, where it protected him from the whip of the wind; and finally the arguments about it with Brigitte. While he was deep in memories of the time he had shared with his raincoat, the minutes flew by, and in Crozon the rain stopped falling.

5

The library was within walking distance. On the way there, Rouche thought about the narrative that had led him to this point. He'd researched the origin of this strange project for amassing rejected manuscripts. He'd gathered information about Jean-Pierre Gourvec. And he'd read Richard Brautigan's *The Abortion*. Rouche was not generally very fond of American literature—apart from Philip Roth. During his days as a critic, he had torn apart Bret Easton Ellis, labelling him "the most overrated writer of the century". What idiocy, he thought now, repentantly, to write such inanities, to try to be so clever with all my definitive, grandiloquent judgements. He didn't regret his opinions, only the way he had expressed them. Sometimes he wished he could rewrite all his articles. So that was Rouche: a man too late to create the best version of himself. The same was true for his relationships; in his head, he had a whole speech written for Brigitte that he'd never had time to give. As he walked towards the library, though, he finally felt as if he were living in the present. He was exactly where he was supposed to be.

Nevertheless, his certainty was quickly proved wrong. There had always been a disconnect between the excitement he felt and the reality of the situation. In other words: the library was closed. A note on the door announced:

Back in a few days.
Thanks for your understanding.

MAGALI CROZE
Manager of the Crozon municipal library

It was exactly like it had been with Joséphine. From the very start of this investigation, every time Rouche wanted to meet a woman, she disappeared before he even got there. Should he see this as a sign? Was it his fault? Perhaps they spread the word, so they wouldn't have to meet him. Added to the fact that Brigitte had just dumped him, this was a lot to take for one man. What should he do now? He absolutely had to talk to the librarian. She could tell him the exact circumstances in which Pick's supposed novel had been discovered. And anyway, he was eager to find out more about Jean-Pierre Gourvec. Rouche felt certain that the dead librarian's past was the key to this mystery.

6

For now, he had to decipher what exactly was meant by "a few days". It was almost as vague as Joséphine's "a while". He went into the neighbouring shops, from the fishmonger's to the stationer's, attempting to obtain information about Magali's return. Nobody knew anything. She'd just left without warning, leaving behind that enigmatic note. Everybody agreed that she was a highly professional person, who worked hard to keep the library alive. From what they said, her sudden vanishing was completely out of character.

At the dry-cleaner's, Rouche spoke to a tall, thin woman who looked like one of Giacometti's sculptures. "Maybe you should ask at the mayor's office?" she suggested.

"You think they'll know when she's coming back?"

"It's a municipal library, so the mayor is her boss. She's bound to have told him. Actually, I'd like to know too. She dropped off a pink suit here, and I'd like to know when she'll be back to pick it up. If you happen to see her, please ask her for me."

"Of course…"

Rouche left, burdened with this message for Magali, although it was highly unlikely that it would be the first thing he said to her when he did manage to find her. He had fallen a long way as a journalist, but not quite so far as to become a messenger boy for a dry-cleaner. A pink suit, indeed…

7

At the mayor's office, a fifty-something secretary explained to him that Magali had left without leaving word of when she would be back.

"Don't you find that worrying?"

"No, she was owed a lot of holiday time. You see, everybody knows everybody here."

"What does that mean?"

"That we all trust one another. I'm not shocked that she should leave without telling the mayor. She works very hard, so she has the right to take a breather."

"But has she ever left like that before, without warning?"

"No, not that I can recall."

"If I may… have you worked here a long time?" asked Rouche.

"Forever. I was an intern here at eighteen, and I never left. I would prefer not to tell you how old I am, but let's just say it's been a while."

"May I ask you another question?"

"Yes."

"Did you know Henri Pick?"

"Vaguely. I know his wife better. We wanted to have a little ceremony for her at the mayor's office, but she refused."

"A ceremony for what?"

"For her husband's book. His novel. Haven't you heard about it?"

"Well, yes, of course. What do you think of all that?"

"All what?"

"That whole story. The novel written by Henri Pick."

"I think it's been wonderful for the town. There are so many visitors now. It's been a big boost for our shopkeepers. If we'd had a publicity office working to promote the town, they could never have achieved what Henri Pick's book did. As for the library, we'll work something out. I have an intern here who could look after it. We wouldn't want to disappoint all our new visitors, would we?"

Rouche paused for a moment to take a good look at this woman. She had such energy. Each of her answers had shot from her mouth as from a catapult of words. He sensed that she could talk for hours like this, answering all sorts of questions with the same tireless vivacity. The point she had just raised was an important one: Rouche had to admit that Crozon had never been as famous as it was now. Perhaps this entire manuscript story had been put together by a brilliant Breton publicist? Abruptly, he asked her: "Did you know Jean-Pierre Gourvec?"

"Why are you asking me that?" said the secretary coldly, her tone suddenly changed.

"Just because. I mean, he was the one who had the idea of the library of rejected books, wasn't he?"

"Oh, ideas. Yes, he had lots of those."

"What do you mean?"

"Nothing. Anyway, if you don't mind, I ought to be getting back to work."

"Okay," said Rouche. Apparently there had been some

awkwardness between Gourvec and this woman. She'd blushed bright red at the mere mention of the librarian's name. After Magali's pink suit, it seemed that his investigation was taking the form of a variety of shades of the same colour. He thanked the secretary warmly for her valuable help and slipped away.

His investigation was not going to make much headway today. He may as well resign himself to it. So what should he do? Go to a bar and drink a few beers? It was an idea, certainly, but perhaps not the most constructive. Then he had a better idea: he would visit Henri Pick.

8

It was true that Magali was not the kind of person to just leave without warning; as a general rule, she was not the kind of person to do anything spontaneous; her existence was a series of planned events.

As she drove home that night, a few days earlier, she had to stop several times. She had to stop and think so she could be certain that she really had experienced what she'd experienced. Her ideas were far from clear (in fact they were totally confused), but a few inhalations was all it took for her to register a strange smell. It was the smell of Jérémie. The reality clung to her skin, the physical proof that it wasn't all a dream. A young man had desired her, in a simple, animal way, and she wondered what she was doing, driving towards her husband

and leaving all that beauty behind. Several times, she wanted to make a U-turn. It was forbidden on that stretch of road marked by a solid white line, but so what? A line couldn't stop her doing what she wanted. And yet she'd continued to drive home, and the journey had seemed to her as long and winding as her own prevarications.

Her husband had called her several times, anxious that she had not yet arrived. She'd made an excuse about doing an inventory. Anybody who knew her even slightly would have guessed that she was lying. But why? Nobody lied in Crozon. There was no reason to. So her husband had worried a little bit, because her absence that evening was unusual, but that was all.

When she got home, Magali prepared an explanation. Perhaps he would notice her mussed hair, her crumpled clothes, the glimmer in her eyes? Yes, José would take one look at her and know exactly what had happened. It was obvious, it was written all over her face, and she had no way of erasing her joy. But everything seemed different that night; she had been surprised by her husband's anxious attitude. Magali had always imagined that she could disappear for at least two or three days before he even noticed her absence. Sometimes they would spend whole evenings without exchanging a single word, and other times their only conversations would be about practical matters: who would do the shopping the next day, for example. Now, she had to admit that she'd been wrong; he'd called her just to find out what she was up to. So what did she want? She might actually have preferred his indifference, so that he wouldn't disturb her pleasure with his phone calls.

She thought about it constantly, that pleasure. The giddiness she'd felt. Jérémie had asked her to come to the library early the next morning and wake him "with her mouth", and she was haunted by those words, but a big part of her thought: he won't be there tomorrow. He said it, but the truth is: he'll be gone. He'll have gone home, or he'll be fucking another woman like me. They couldn't be too hard to find; there were women like her everywhere, women who couldn't bear not being touched any more, women who thought they were fat and hideous. Yes, everywhere he went, he must leave behind beautiful, indestructible memories; that was his legacy, since he wasn't able to get published. Yes, she felt certain now; he wouldn't be there. She smiled at the fact that she'd ever imagined he would be.

At home, she walked silently across the living room. Magali was surprised to find all the lights off. This was not at all the setting for a deeply worried man. She tiptoed up to their bedroom, where she found her husband, mouth open, deep in a fathomless slumber.

9

For much of that night, Magali was wide awake. She left early the next morning, after spending an hour in the bathroom. She hadn't needed to explain anything, since her husband had been asleep the whole time she'd been in the house. He'd be happy when he woke up, anyway, because the coffee was hot and the table set for breakfast.

In the dawn light, she opened the door of the library. Inside, all was calm, as if the books too were sleeping. She walked between the shelves to her office, her heart beating in a strange new rhythm. She could have walked quickly, could have rushed towards what she was going to find, but she liked this waiting period; for a few more metres, for a few more seconds, everything was still possible. Jérémie could be there, sleeping, waiting to be woken by her mouth. She gently opened the door and saw the young man lying on the floor, sleeping as calmly as the surface of a Swiss lake. She closed the door, and opened it again, as if to be certain that it wasn't an optical illusion. Then she moved towards him, to take a closer look. The night before, she hadn't dared really look at him, often turning away when their eyes met. Now, she could contemplate him, pausing over every detail of his body, intoxicated by his beauty. So… now she had to wake him with her mouth. Did he want kisses? She started touching her lips softly to his chest, then his stomach, and he shivered; he put his hand on her head then, caressing her hair for an instant, before gently pushing her a little lower.

Later, Magali made a coffee and handed it to Jérémie. He was sitting behind the desk. He must have wandered around the library during the night, because he'd assembled a little pile of books. Among other names, Magali spotted Kafka, Kerouac and Kundera. From this, she could have concluded that he only looked at the K section. He hesitated for a moment between *The Dharma Bums* and *The Trial*, before finally opening *Laughable Loves*. Magali watched him for a moment, then asked: "Are you hungry? Shall I get us some croissants?"

"No, thanks. I have everything I need right here," he said, gesturing at his book.

She left him alone, so she could open the library to customers. It was a particularly quiet day, which gave Magali plentiful opportunities to go and see Jérémie. Sometimes he would tell her to come over, and he would slide his hand between her legs. She let him do it without saying anything. What was going to happen? What did he want? How long was he going to stay? She would have liked to simply enjoy the madness, but that was impossible: her mind was filled with an avalanche of questions. Jérémie no longer seemed like the tortured dropout he had the day before; today, he was more like a bon vivant, enjoying life's gifts. At the end of the day, she went out to buy a bottle of wine and some food and they picnicked on the floor. They talked more than they had the first night. Jérémie told her about his difficult relationship with his parents, and his mother in particular; he'd been sent to boarding school, then put in a home, and now it was almost five years since he'd seen them. "They might be dead," he said, before admitting that this was unlikely; someone would have told him if they'd died. Magali was chilled by this idea. When she saw young people begging outside the supermarket, she always suspected that family problems were at the root of their homelessness. She thought about her daughters: she didn't see them often enough. Perhaps she didn't show them enough of her love.

Encouraged by Jérémie, Magali started talking about her own parents. They had died many years ago, and she never spoke about them any more. Nobody ever asked her about her childhood. Suddenly she was seized by an intense emotion. For years, she had lived without asking herself what was missing in her life. She understood now that she had been suffering from the lack of her mother's closeness. She had told herself that her mother's death was *just one of those things*. Now she realized that just because something was a common experience didn't mean that you couldn't feel it as an emotional outrage, something it would be impossible to ever get over.

She put words to the chasm inside her, and even an explanation—about the way she'd let go of her body. Jérémie sensed her distress and consoled her with a few touches.

10

The days that followed were all suffused in the same atmosphere. Magali flitted between moments of euphoria, when she was electrified by the power of her feelings, and moments of dread at what was happening. She tried to avoid her husband, which wasn't very difficult. Recently, José had been more exhausted than usual by his working hours at the Renault factory. He was full-time now. In order to maintain car production in France, the employees had to redouble their efforts, show that their expertise was more valuable than low-cost manpower abroad. The consequence of this fierce competition was an ever-greater exploitation of all workers: those who wanted to keep their jobs, and those who hoped to get one. Both sides lost. José was looking forward to his early retirement as if to a release from prison. Finally, he would be able to enjoy life; in other words, go fishing and walk around the coast. Perhaps his wife might even go with him sometimes; it had been ages since they'd spent time together like that, without any objective in mind, just wandering around aimlessly.

Jérémie was still sleeping in the office; Magali had brought him a blanket. The lack of comfort did not seem to bother him. She didn't dare ask him how long he was planning to stay. Until, one day, he announced: "I have to go home."

"When?"

"Tomorrow."

"..."

"I'll get the train to Paris. I'll probably spend one night there, and on Sunday I'll leave for Lyons. A friend of mine has offered me a part-time job. I can't turn it down. You understand?"

"Yes. I understand."

"I have a small attic room in Lyons. It's pretty tiny, but it's fine. You could come."

"Come... with you?"

"Yeah. What's stopping you?"

"Well... everything."

"You don't want to stay with me?"

"Of course I do. That's not the point. I mean, I have a job…"

"Just close the library. Tell them you're taking sick leave. And with your experience, I'm sure you'd find something in Lyons."

"What about my husband?"

"You don't love him any more. And your children have grown up. We'll be happy there. There's something special between us. It was my fate to bring my book here, so I could meet you. Nobody has ever been so kind to me before."

"But I haven't done anything special."

"The past week has been the best of my life: lying here, with these books, and you coming to see me from time to time. And I love making love with you. Don't you?"

"I… yes."

"So? Let's go tomorrow."

"But… this is all happening too quickly."

"Does that matter? You'll regret it if you don't come."

Magali had to sit down. Jérémie had spoken very calmly, as if what he was saying was simple and obvious, whereas for her it meant overturning her entire life. She started thinking: he's right, I should just leave, I shouldn't even think about it, because it's obvious, I can't let this man slip away from me, I can't live without his body, his kisses, his beauty, I couldn't just go on with my life knowing that he was somewhere far away, yes, Jérémie is right, I don't love my husband any more, or in any case I never question my feelings when I'm with him, it's just the way it is, and it will go on like that until death, what Jérémie is offering me is the chance to escape for a moment from the death that awaits me, he's offering me life and I'm suffocating, I can't breathe any more amid all these books, they're stifling me, all these stories that are preventing me from living my own story, all these sentences, all these words, weighing me down all these years, I'm tired of novels, I'm tired of readers, I'm tired of failed writers, I can't stand these books any more, I need to escape the prison of these shelves, calm down, Magali, calm down, everybody gets like this after a while, we all feel a sort of disgust for our life, our job, but I love books, I loved José, and I probably still love him if I'm honest, it would make me feel bad to just leave him here, orphaned, but it's true that we don't do much together any more, he's become a mere presence, a constant presence, changeless and indistinct, united as we are by our past, our memories, that's maybe the most important thing, the memories that prove that love existed, and we have the physical proof with our sons, my children who have moved away, before I was everything for them and now it's just a few quick calls, mechanical tenderness, hellos that are like goodbyes, how would they react if I left, one would say it's my life, the other that I was mad to do that to Papa, but in the end I don't care about their opinions, I don't judge them for the choices they make, so they should respect my choices too, leave me free to try to be happy.

I I

Again, Magali didn't get much sleep. She thought about Henri Pick's book. It seemed to have incredible resonance in her own life. Who had she been living with these last few hours? With Jérémie or with José? That night, she observed her husband, the way you might contemplate a landscape on the last day of your holiday. She wanted to memorize everything. He was sleeping deeply, completely unaware of the emotional danger that prowled close by. Everything was confused at that moment, but Magali knew one thing: she couldn't go on living as she had before.

The next day, she left without waking him. It was a Saturday, he didn't have work; he would sleep until noon at least. As soon as she entered the library, Jérémie asked her what she'd decided. She thought she would have a few more seconds to think it over, but no: the time had come to take the plunge.

"I'm going to go home early this afternoon…" she began, then stopped talking.

"Yeah. And then?"

"I'll pick up my things. And then we'll leave together."

"Perfect," said Jérémie, moving towards her.

"Wait. Wait. Let me finish," said Magali, raising her hand to order him back.

"All right."

"I checked. The bus to Quimper is at three o'clock. After that, we'll take the 5.12 train to Paris."

"You've researched it all. That's great."

"…"

"But why don't we just go in your car? It'd be more practical."

"I can't do that. My husband's car broke down months

221

ago. He'd have to buy another one, and that would be too expensive. He goes to the factory with a colleague who picks him up and drops him off. Anyway, you get the idea... I can't leave him *and* take the car."

"Yeah, you're right."

"..."

"Can I hold you in my arms now?" Jérémie asked.

I 2

All morning long, Magali forced herself to work *as if nothing was happening*. She'd always liked that expression, the way it tried to mask the essential; in this case, the precipice of a life-changing decision. Several times, she went to see Jérémie, who seemed lost in thought.[21] He must be mentally constructing novels that he will never finish, she thought; so many lives are soothed by illusions. Whenever she glanced at him, she had to admit in her heart of hearts that it was folly to go with him. After all, she barely knew him. But she was living through one of those rare moments when *after* doesn't matter; when only the power of *now* guides your life. She felt good with him, it was as simple as that. There was no point trying to define what was happening in her body; words were useless in this kind of situation. No matter how many of the thousands of

21 He was the kind of man whom you always feel that you are disturbing, even though he's not actually doing anything.

books surrounding her she opened, she would never find the key to her own behaviour.

Around noon, as the library was emptying, she said to Jérémie: "I'm going to close up. You should go to the bus station now, and I'll meet you there later when I've picked up my things."

"Perfect. Can I take a few books?" he asked casually, as if completely unaware of how important this moment was to Magali.

"Yes, of course. You can take anything you want."

"Just two or three novels. I want to travel lightly, since we're not taking the car."

He gathered his belongings, took three books, and the two of them left the library. Out of fear that someone would see them, they separated without any show of affection.

13

Magali headed straight for her bedroom. Her husband was still asleep, which proved how exhausted he was. For a moment, she sat on the edge of the bed, and you might have thought that she was going to wake him; you might have thought that she was going to tell him everything. She could have told him: I met another man, and I have no choice, I have to leave you because I'll die if I let him leave and he never touches me again. But she didn't say anything. She just kept watching him, taking care not to make a sound so as not to disturb his sleep.

She examined their bedroom. She knew every inch of it by heart. There were no surprises here; even the gathering of dust took place at the same, predictable rhythm. This was the familiar framework of her existence, and she was almost surprised at how reassured it made her feel. While the last few days had been divine in terms of pleasure, they had also been exhausting. She had lived each minute of her brief passion with her stomach in knots, dreading the possibility that she would be judged for her actions. It was perhaps predictable with José, but she was beginning to realize that there was a form of pleasure in that predictability. There was a beauty in this comfort. What had seemed to her mediocre was now revealed in another light, and her life itself looked different. She understood that she was going to miss what she had rejected a week ago. Yes, with a certain irony, at this last moment, she felt herself missing what she was about to leave. Tears ran down her cheeks, releasing all the feelings that had been pent up inside her since she first found herself in this emotional whirlwind.

Finally she stood up, grabbed a bag and threw a few things inside. Opening a drawer, she woke her husband.

"What are you doing?"

"Nothing. Just tidying up."

"That's not what it looks like. You're packing a bag."

"A bag?"

"Yes. Are you going somewhere?"

"No."

"So what are you doing?"

"I don't know."

"You don't know?"

"…"

"You look like you're crying. Are you sure you're okay?"

Magali couldn't move. She had forgotten how to breathe. José watched her uncomprehendingly. Could he possibly imagine that a man young enough to be his son was waiting for his wife at the bus station? He usually didn't even notice Magali's mood swings. When he didn't understand her, he just thought *oh well, that's women for you*. But this time, he sat up in bed. He had sensed something different, perhaps serious.

"Tell me what you're doing."

"…"

"You can tell me."

"I'm packing a bag, because I want us to leave now. Straight away. Please don't ask questions."

"But… where are we going?"

"I don't care. Let's just get in the car and go. The two of us. For a few days. It's been years since we went anywhere on holiday."

"But I can't just leave. What about my job?"

"I told you, I don't care. You can get a doctor's note. You haven't been off sick in thirty years. Please, don't think about it."

"So that's what you were doing with the bag?"

"Yes, I was packing our stuff."

"What about the library?"

"I'll leave a note on the door. Come on, get dressed. We're leaving."

"But I haven't had my coffee yet."

"Please. Let's just go. Come on. Quickly, quickly, quickly. You can get a coffee on the motorway."

"…"

14

A few minutes later, they were in the car. José had never seen his wife like this, and he realized that he just needed to do what she said. She was right, after all. He couldn't keep going like this. His job was killing him. It was time to go, to leave everything behind, to take a breather, if they wanted to survive. On the way, she stopped at the library and left a note explaining that she'd be back in a few days. She drove quickly, without really knowing where she was going, intoxicated by that uncertainty. At last, she was acting spontaneously. José opened the window to let the wind whip his face. He wanted to be sure that he really was awake, because what he was living through at that moment felt like a dream.

15

Without knowing it, Rouche had seen Jérémie at the bus station that day. Then he'd seen that the library was closed, and asked a few shopkeepers about it before questioning a woman at the mayor's office. This had led to a dead end, as was becoming usual with this investigation. He always failed first before finding what he was looking for. In fact, it was the succession of failures that had led him to where he found himself now: on the right track.

He was beginning to understand why his life had forced him to face up to such massive disillusionment; he'd imagined he was living it the way he wanted to, and he'd headed into literary spheres armed with strategic ideas for success. Now he was discovering that he should also follow his intuition. That was why he'd felt the need to visit Henri Pick's grave. From there, he could follow the thread back towards the truth buried deep in the past.

The journalist was surprised by how big Crozon's cemetery was; hundreds of graves either side of a central aisle that ended in a monument for the victims of both world wars. At the entrance, there was a small hut, painted a faded pink, where the concierge lived. Seeing Rouche appear, the man emerged from his lair: "You looking for Pick?"

"Yes," replied Rouche, a little taken aback.

"Space M64."

"Ah, thank you…"

The man went back into his hut without another word. Apparently he was an information minimalist. He came out, said M64, and went back in. "M64," Rouche mentally repeated several times, before thinking: even dead people have an address.

He walked slowly through the rows of graves, not looking for their numbers, preferring to decipher each name until he found that of Henri Pick. Instinctively, he started calculating the number of years that each person had lived. Laurent Joncour (1939–2005) had died early, at sixty-six. He wasn't the only one, and the journalist could not help thinking that all of them, like him, had lived ordinary lives; each corpse had, on one day or another, made love for the first time, argued with a friend over something that now seemed stupid… perhaps some of them had also scratched cars. Here, he was a survivor of the human community. And, a few metres away, he now spotted a fellow survivor. She was a woman in her fifties, and there was something familiar about her. He walked towards her, while continuing to read the names on the graves, but he felt almost certain that this woman was standing at Pick's grave.

16

When he came closer, Rouche recognized Joséphine. He'd waited for her outside her shop, in vain, and now he'd found her here. He glanced at the grave and saw a heap of flowers and even a few letters. This vision gave him a real sense of the phenomenon that had grown around the novelist. Pick's daughter remained immobile in front of the plot, in a sort of trance. She didn't notice the new visitor. Unlike the photographs of her he'd seen in the press, where she smiled so excitedly that it bordered on the ridiculous, she looked serious now. Of course, she was standing by her father's grave, but Rouche knew that the source of her sadness lay elsewhere. In fact, he thought, she had come here to seek a comfort that she couldn't find beyond the cemetery's walls.

"Your father wrote you a very beautiful letter," he said with a sigh.

"Excuse me?" said Joséphine, surprised to find a man standing next to her.

"The letter that you found. It's very moving."

"But… how do you know that? Who are you?"

"Jean-Michel Rouche. I'm a journalist. Don't worry. I wanted to meet you in Rennes, but you'd disappeared. Mathilde told me about the letter. I managed to persuade her to show it to me."

"Why would you do that?"

"I was looking for a written trace… of your father."

"Look, leave me in peace. Can't you see that I'm busy?"

"…"

Rouche took a few steps back, then stopped as if frozen. What an idiot he had been not to anticipate this sort of reaction. He was so tactless! This woman was visiting her father's grave, and he talked to her like that, out of the blue, about the letter. About that very personal letter which he had obtained without her permission. How did he expect her to react? His investigation made him happy, but he hated the idea of hurting someone. Sensing that he was still standing behind her, Joséphine turned. She might easily have become annoyed again, but something disarmed her. With his frayed, soaked raincoat, this man looked like some sad, harmless lunatic. She asked him: "What do you want exactly?"

"I'm not sure this is the right moment."

"Oh, stop beating about the bush. Just say what you have to say."

"I have a hunch that it wasn't your father who wrote that novel."

"Oh really? Why?"

"Just a hunch. Something seemed off to me."

"Go on."

"I needed proof. Written evidence."

"So that's why you wanted the letter?"

"Yes."

"Well, now you've seen it. How does it help you?"

"You know very well how it helps me."

"What do you mean?"

"You can't lie to yourself. All you'd have to do is read two lines of that letter to realize that your father could never have written a novel."

"…"

"It's a touching letter, but the vocabulary is very limited, the style is naïve, it's full of mistakes… I mean, don't you agree?"

"…"

"You can tell that it took him a superhuman effort to write you those words, because he knew that all children receive letters from their parents when they're away at holiday camps."

"A quickly dashed-off letter to a child and a novel… it's hardly the same thing."

"Be honest. You know as well as I do that your father couldn't have written a novel."

"I don't know that. And how can you ever be sure? We can't ask him any more."

They both looked at Henri Pick's gravestone, but nothing happened.

17

One hour later, Rouche was in Madeleine's living room, sipping a cup of caramel tea. Joséphine was living here for the moment, he guessed, while she recovered from the trauma of Marc's betrayal. She was trying to find some serenity in her life, to rebuild herself. She only left the house to go to the cemetery. And yet, she resented her father. His novel had sown destruction, in the end. Madeleine said that her ex-son-in-law's unspeakable actions should allow her daughter to finally turn the page. And she was right, of course. The brutality of Joséphine's discovery had put an end to years of sorrow; now she was mourning the death of all hope that she would be able to revive her marriage.

Marc had sent her lots of messages, apologising, attempting to explain. He'd been deep in debt, and the other woman had coerced him into it. He didn't know how he could have acted so unscrupulously. Since then, he had really broken up with her. He wrote to Joséphine about their reunion: while his motivations had initially been bad ones, he'd felt such intense happiness at being with her again. He knew he'd ruined everything, but he couldn't forget the joy of their rekindled relationship. He saw everything clearly now. And it was too late. Joséphine would never see him again.

For now, she was sitting in a corner of the living room, at a distance from Rouche and his mother. Madeleine reread the copy of the letter several times, before asking: "What do you want me to say?"

"Whatever you want."

"My husband wrote a novel. That's just how it is. It was his secret."

"But the letter…"

"What about it?"

"It's obvious that he couldn't write. Don't you think?"

"Oh, I'm so tired of all this. Everybody's gone crazy over this book. Look at my poor daughter! It's all such nonsense. I'm going to call the editor."

Rouche watched in surprise as Madeleine rose to pick up the telephone. She opened an old, dog-eared black notebook and dialled Delphine's number.

It was almost eight in the evening; Delphine was eating dinner with Frédéric. Madeleine did not waste words: "There's a journalist at my house. He says Henri didn't write the book. We found a letter."

"A letter?"

"Yes. Not very well written… When you read it, you have to doubt that he wrote a novel."

"But… a letter and a novel… it's hardly the same thing," Delphine stammered. "And who's the journalist? Is it Rouche?"

"Does it matter? Just tell me the truth."

"But… the truth is that your husband's name was on the manuscript. And the contract is in your name. You will receive all the royalties. Isn't that proof enough that I've always believed that he was the author?"

Delphine had put the phone on loudspeaker, so that Frédéric could hear the conversation. He whispered: "Tell her to ask the journalist who he thinks the author is." The old lady repeated this question, and Rouche replied: "I have an idea. But I can't say anything for now. In any case, it's time to stop letting people believe that it was Henri Pick." Delphine tried to smooth things over by telling Madeleine that, until there was any proof to the contrary, the author of the novel was her husband. And this journalist should find some real evidence to back up his theories instead of digging up old letters sent to a child. She added: "If you found an old shopping list written by Proust, maybe you'd think it was impossible that the same man had written *In Search of Lost Time*!" With this, she wished Madeleine a good evening and hung up.

Frédéric pretended to applaud. "Bravo! Excellent argument. Proust's shopping list…"

"It just came to me."

"Anyway, you knew this was bound to happen one day."

"Doubt is normal. But that letter doesn't prove that Pick didn't write his book. There's no concrete proof."

"For now…" added Frédéric, with a smile that Delphine found supremely irritating. She was usually so level-headed, but she flew off the handle now.

"What's that supposed to mean? My reputation is at stake here! The book is a success, and everybody thinks I have a gift, so that's it. This stops here."

"This stops here?"

"Yes! The story is perfect as it is!" she said, getting to her feet. Frédéric tried to grab her arm, but she pushed him away. She rushed over to the door and left the apartment.

Madeleine's call had revived tensions between them. They didn't agree, but before they had at least been able to talk about it; why had she reacted so violently? He ran after her. Out in the street, he looked around, and was surprised to see that she was already quite far off. Yet he had the impression that he'd waited only a few seconds before going after her. Increasingly, his sense of time seemed distorted, the result of a disconnect between the motions of his mind and the reality of the present. Sometimes he would spend a long moment thinking about a sentence, and he'd be disconcerted to discover that two hours had passed. He was losing touch with everyday life, and the sensation was growing stronger as he drew closer to the end of his novel. It was so long and so hard that the final chapters had been written in a kind of fog. *The Man Who Told the Truth* would soon be finished.

He started running after Delphine. In the middle of the street, in front of numerous witnesses, he grabbed her by the arm.

"Let me go!" she cried out.

"No, you're coming home with me. This is nonsense. We should be able to talk, without it degenerating like this."

"I know what you're going to say, and I don't agree."

"I've never seen you like this before. What's going on?"

"…"

"Delphine? Answer me."

"…"

"Did you meet someone else?"

"No."

"Then what is it?"

"I'm pregnant."

PART XIII

PART NINE

AFTER HANGING UP the phone, Madeleine showed her contract to Rouche. It was true: she was due to receive 10 per cent royalties, which would be a considerable sum. So the editor really must believe that Pick was the novel's author. Continuing their discussion, Madeleine and Joséphine admitted that they had been seduced by this rather mad idea. They had believed it but, deep inside, they had always thought the story a little improbable.

"So who did write the book?" Joséphine demanded.

"I have an idea," admitted Rouche.

"Tell us, then!" Madeleine urged him.

"All right. I'll tell you what I think, but first, could I have a little more of your delicious caramel tea?"

"…"

2

When everybody began talking about the Pick phenomenon, several journalists became interested in the fate of such rejected books. They wanted to find out who had turned down *The Last*

Hours of a Love Affair. Perhaps they would uncover a reader's report justifying the rejection? Of course, there was still the possibility that the Breton pizzeria owner had never sent his novel to publishers. He could have written it, without showing it to anyone, before fate had decreed that the library of rejects was created in his own home town. At that point, he'd decided to deposit his manuscript there. It was a plausible hypothesis, and many people had admired the qualities of a man who had never sought the limelight. But the journalists still wanted to check whether he'd sent his novel to any publishers. And there was no trace of it anywhere.

In truth, most publishers do not keep archives listing the books they have rejected; the only exception is Julliard, who famously published Françoise Sagan's *Bonjour Tristesse*. In Julliard's basement was a list of all the books they had received over the past fifty years; dozens of files with rows of author names and book titles. Several newspapers sent interns to go through that list of rejects. There was no mention of Pick. But Rouche, guided by his intuition, had searched for another name: Gourvec. Had the librarian himself written a book that nobody wanted? Perhaps he had personal reasons for putting so much energy into creating a library of rejects? This was Rouche's theory, and he found the evidence to support it: on three occasions—in 1962, 1974 and 1976—Gourvec had tried to publish a novel and had probably sent it to several publishers, including Julliard. They had all said no. These failures had surely pained him, because no trace of him could be found after this. He had given up trying to be published.

When Rouche had discovered evidence of the novels rejected by Julliard, he had done some research into Gourvec's estate. No children, no material goods; he had left nothing behind. Nobody would ever know that he had written anything. He had probably got rid of all his manuscripts; all, except one. This was what Rouche imagined. When he created this library, Gourvec had decided to slip one of his own books onto its shelves. Naturally, he didn't want to put his name to it. So he'd chosen the most insignificant person in the town to represent him: Henri Pick. It was a symbolic choice, a way of giving form to his text through a shadowy presence. According to Rouche, this was undoubtedly how it had happened.

Gourvec was well known for giving away books: it was entirely possible that he had one day given Henri a copy of *Yevgeny Onegin*. The pizzeria owner, unused to such presents, had been touched by this gesture and had kept the novel all his life. He wasn't a reader, though, so he'd never opened the book, and therefore had no idea that certain phrases had been underlined:

> To live and think is to be daunted,
> To feel contempt for other men.
> To feel is to be hurt, and haunted
> By days that will not come again,
> With a lost sense of charm and wonder,
> And memory to suffer under—
> The stinging serpent of remorse.
> This all adds piquancy, of course,
> To conversation.

Those lines might evoke the end of a literary dream. Whoever writes has a heart that beats. Once hope has been shattered, it turns to the bitterness of the unfulfilled. And then to the sting of remorse.

Before going in search of Gourvec's past, Rouche had decided to start his investigation by finding proof that Pick was not the book's author. This was the first, critical stage. He'd gone to Rennes, and discovered the letter. And now he was in Crozon, at the Picks' house, explaining to them what he thought. To his surprise, the mother and daughter seemed to have little trouble accepting his theory. Although another factor had to be taken into consideration: both of them had suffered unpleasant, even tragic, consequences as a result of the book's publication. They wanted to get back to their old lives and felt generally quite relieved by the idea that Henri had never written a novel. Later, it occurred to Joséphine that this revelation might prevent them receiving the royalties; but, at that moment, they only considered the emotional aspect.

"So you think it was Gourvec who wrote my husband's novel?" asked Madeleine.

"Yes."

"How do you plan to prove it?" asked Joséphine.

"Well, as I said, it's only a theory at the moment. And Gourvec left nothing behind—no manuscript, no admission of his passion for writing. Gourvec rarely talked about himself; Magali mentioned that in an interview."

"All Breton men are like that. There are no chatterboxes

here. You didn't choose the right region for an investigation," said Madeleine, amused.

"Very true. But I have a feeling that there's still something about this story that I haven't grasped yet."

"What?"

"When I mentioned Gourvec at the mayor's office, the secretary blushed bright red. And then she became very unfriendly."

"So?"

"I thought maybe she'd had an affair with Gourvec, and that it ended badly."

"Just like with his wife," added Madeleine, unaware that this response would change everything.

3

It was very late, and even if Rouche would have liked to keep talking—and, in particular, questioning Madeleine about what she'd said regarding Gourvec's wife—he sensed that it would be better to postpone the rest of their discussion until the following day. As in Rennes, swept along by his enthusiasm, he had failed to book a hotel room. And this time he didn't even have a car to sleep in. Out of politeness, he asked his hosts if they knew of a hotel in the area; but it was practically midnight, and everything was closed. Clearly he would end up spending the night in their house, but he felt embarrassed at not having planned anything, and at imposing himself in such an inelegant manner. Madeleine reassured him, adding that it would be her pleasure.

"The only problem is that the sofa bed's in a terrible state. I would advise against it. So that only leaves my daughter's room. There are two beds in there."

"My room?" repeated Joséphine.

"I can sleep on the sofa. My back already hates me, so this won't change our relationship one iota. Please don't worry about it…"

"No, it'll be better with Joséphine," insisted Madeleine, who seemed strangely fond of Rouche. She loved the child that she still saw within him.

Joséphine led Rouche to her room, and showed him the two single beds. It was her childhood bedroom, unchanged since those days; she used to invite her friends to sleepovers in the extra bed. The two beds were separated by a small table, on which stood a lamp with an orange shade. It was easy to imagine children chatting the night away against such a backdrop, sharing secrets. But here, now, they were two adults of the same age, each sunk in solitude, like two parallel lines. They started talking about their lives, and the conversation lasted a while.

When Joséphine turned off the lamp, Rouche noticed that the ceiling was scattered with luminous stars.

4

They woke at almost the same instant. Joséphine took advantage of the darkness to slip into the bathroom. Rouche was thinking that he hadn't slept this well in a long time; presumably a consequence of the fatigue accumulated over recent days and the quietness of this house. There was another feeling inside him too, although it was not something he could define. In truth, he felt lighter than he had the previous day, as if a weight had been lifted from his shoulders. Probably the weight of the break-up with Brigitte. You can rationalize everything, but it is always your body that decides how long it takes an emotional wound to heal. That morning, when he opened his eyes, he felt able to breathe again. The pain had vanished.

5

Over breakfast, Madeleine talked about Gourvec's wife. She hadn't stayed long in Crozon, but they'd got to know each other quite well. And for one simple reason: Marina—that was her name—had worked as a waitress at the Picks' pizzeria.

"It was when I was pregnant," said Madeleine in a neutral tone that gave nothing away of the tragedy behind those words.[22]

"Gourvec's wife worked with your husband?"

"Yes, for two or three weeks. And then she left. She broke up with Jean-Pierre and went back to live in Paris, I think. I never heard from her after that."

Rouche was stunned; he'd thought Gourvec had chosen Pick's name for his manuscript almost at random, to avoid

22 Madeleine had lost a child at birth, a few years before she had Joséphine.

having to invent a pseudonym. Now he was discovering a connection between the two men.

"So your husband knew her better than you did?"

"Why do you say that?"

"Well, you just told me you were pregnant, and she was replacing you."

"I couldn't work any more, but I was there practically every day. And it was mostly me she talked to."

"And what did she tell you?"

"She was a fragile woman, who was hoping she'd finally found somewhere she could be happy. She said it was hard to be a German in France in the 1950s."

"She was German?"

"Yes, although you couldn't really tell. I think most people had no idea. I only knew because she told me. You could tell she was damaged in some way. But I don't know much more than that. Or I don't remember much more, anyway."

"How did she end up here?"

"It started with letters. She and Gourvec were pen pals. It was pretty common at the time. She told me he wrote such beautiful letters. So she decided to marry him and come and live here."

"Ah, so he wrote beautiful letters," Rouche repeated. "I have to find that woman and take a look at those letters. It could be crucial..."

"Is it really that important for you to prove that my father didn't write that book?" Joséphine asked in a cutting voice that dampened Rouche's enthusiasm.

He didn't know what to say. After a brief silence, he said that he was obsessed with finding out the true identity of the novel's author. It was hard to explain. He'd felt completely empty after his professional disappointments. He'd tried to put on a front, to smile occasionally, to shake hands, but it was as if death was slowly taking possession of his body. Until the moment when, unaccountably, he'd been woken from his depression by this story. He felt sure that something was waiting for him at the end of this adventure, something that would give him a reason to live. That was why he wanted proof, even if everything strongly suggested that Gourvec was the author. The two women were taken aback by this monologue, but Joséphine went on: "And what will you do with your proof?"

"I don't know," Rouche replied.

"Listen, darling," Madeleine told her daughter, "it's important for us, too, to know. I mean, I went on television to talk about your father's novel. I'd like to know the truth before I die."

"Don't say that, Mama," said Joséphine, taking her mother's hand.

Rouche couldn't know, but Joséphine's gesture was something that had become a rare event lately. As was Madeleine calling her daughter "darling". Unexpectedly, recent events had brought them closer together. They had both been thrust into the limelight, with often paradoxical consequences: simultaneously happy and disappointing, intoxicating and unbearable. Joséphine ended up seeing it her mother's way. The truth that Rouche would uncover was perhaps necessary for their peace of mind. He would go off in search of Marina, who would surely be able to confirm that Gourvec was the secret genius behind *The Last Hours of a Love Affair*. He would also discover the reasons for their abrupt separation after only a few weeks of marriage.

6

Early that afternoon, Joséphine drove Rouche to Rennes; from there, he would take the train to Paris. As for her, she went back to work the following morning, after a few days off.

7

Since the break-up with Brigitte, Rouche had gone back to living in his attic room. That Sunday evening, he was alone, in its cramped confines, fifty years old, with grave financial difficulties, and yet he was happy. Happiness is always relative; several years before, if someone had shown him this vision of the future, he would have been terrified. But after all he had been through, he could see this tiny hovel as a sort of paradise.

Before leaving, he'd asked Madeleine for a favour: would she go to the mayor's office on Monday morning and check the marriage register. She had known Marina only under her married name, Gourvec. But after leaving Crozon, it was likely that she had used her maiden name again. On the internet, Rouche had found no trace of a Marina Gourvec.

Madeleine was confronted by the same woman Rouche had seen two days before. She explained her request, and the woman replied: "Why is everybody so obsessed with Gourvec at the moment?"

"It's not an obsession. It's just that I knew his wife, and I was hoping to find her again."

"Oh really? He was married? First I've heard of it. I thought he was against commitment."

Martine Paimpec said a few more things about the librarian that left no room for doubt: the two of them had known each other very well indeed. Without being prompted, she ended up opening her heart and pouring out all the regrets that had festered for so long inside it. Madeleine wasn't surprised: Gourvec was well known for living with his books and for not loving anything or anyone else. She tried to comfort the woman: "It wasn't you. In my opinion, it's wise to be wary of anyone who loves books. At least I didn't have to worry about that, with Henri."

"But he wrote a book…"

"Maybe not. In fact, it might have been Gourvec who wrote it. And, frankly, a writer who would put my husband's name on his book… what a weirdo! So you have nothing to regret."

"…"

Martine wondered if she could consider these words as a consolation; it didn't really matter any more, after all. He'd been dead for a long time, and she still loved him.

*

After a while, Madeleine found the information she was looking for: Marina's maiden name was Brücke.

*

Two hours later, Rouche was squeezed into one corner of his
room in an attempt to find a Wi-Fi signal. He was squatting
on his third-floor neighbour's network, but it only worked if
he pressed himself against the wall. He quickly found traces
of several different Marina Brückes, but they were mostly
Facebook profiles, with photographs of women who were too
young to be the one he was searching for. Finally, he found
a link to a record cover, on which the following dedication
was printed:

> To Marina, my mother.
> So that she can see me.

The search engine had found the words "Marina" and "Brücke"
on that page. The record in question was by a young pianist,
Hugo Brücke, who'd recorded Schubert's *Hungarian Melodies*.
That name was vaguely familiar to Rouche: at one time,
he'd gone to a lot of concerts and operas. It struck him
that he hadn't listened to music in a long time, and that he
missed it. He looked for more information on this Brücke,
and discovered that he was playing a concert in Paris the
next day.

8

The show was sold out, so he waited in a narrow backstreet where the artist was supposed to come out after the concert. Next to him stood a very small woman whose age he couldn't guess. She walked over to him: "Do you like Hugo Brücke too?"

"Yes."

"I've been to all his concerts. In Cologne, last year, it was divine."

"So why didn't you go tonight?" Rouche asked.

"I never buy a ticket when he plays in Paris. It's a matter of principle."

"I don't understand."

"He lives here, so it's not as good. Hugo doesn't play the same way in his own city. When he's away, it's different. I came to realize that. The difference is tiny, but I can hear it. And he knows it, because I'm his biggest fan. I have my picture taken with him after every concert, but when he's in Paris I just wait outside the exit."

"So you think he plays less well in Paris?"

"I didn't say 'less well'. It's just different. In terms of intensity. And yes, I told him that, and he's intrigued. You really have to know his music to its depths to sense the difference."

"That's surprising. So you're his biggest fan, huh?"

"Yes."

"Then you probably know that he dedicated his last record to Marina…"

"Of course. That's his mother."

"And there was a rather enigmatic message too: 'So that she can see me'."

"That's lovely."

"Is it because she's dead?"

"No, not at all. She sometimes comes to see him. Well, to hear him anyway. She's blind."

"Ah…"

"They're very close. He visits her almost every day."

"Where does she live?"

"In a retirement home, in Montmartre. It's called The Light. Her son got her a room with a view of the Sacré-Coeur."

"You said she was blind."

"So? Eyes are not the only way of seeing," the small woman countered.

Rouche looked at her and tried to smile, but he couldn't manage it. She wanted to ask him why he was asking all these questions, but she didn't. As the journalist had gathered all the information he was seeking, he thanked her and left.

A few minutes later, Hugo Brücke came out and, once again, had his picture taken with his biggest fan.

9

The next morning, Rouche penetrated the beating heart of that building named The Light. It seemed like a symbolic name for the end of his investigation. A woman at the reception desk asked him the reason for his visit, and he explained that he wished to meet Marina Brücke.

"Are you a relative?" the woman asked.

"No, not exactly. I'm a friend of her husband."

"She's not married."

"No, but she was. A long time ago. Just tell her I'm a friend of Jean-Pierre Gourvec."

While the woman went upstairs to see Marina, Rouche waited in the middle of a large lobby where he saw several elderly women. They waved to him as they passed. He had the impression that they did not consider him a visitor, but a newly arrived resident.

The receptionist returned and offered to take him to Marina's room. In the doorway, he saw Marina from behind. She was sitting at the window, which did indeed have a view of the Sacré-Coeur. The old woman swivelled her wheelchair to face her visitor.

"Hello, madame," said Rouche.

"Hello, monsieur. You can put your coat on my bed."

"Thank you."

"You should change it, you know."

"Sorry?"

"Your raincoat. It's very old."

"But… how could you…?" Rouche stammered, incredulous.

"Don't worry, I'm just joking."

"Joking?"

"Yes. Roselyne at reception always tells me something about my visitors. It's a game we play. This time, she told me: 'His raincoat is really old and worn.'"

"Ah… I see. Yes. It's a little scary, but it is funny."

"So you're a friend of Jean-Pierre?"

"Yes."

"How is he?"

"I'm sorry to tell you this, but… he died several years ago."

Marina did not respond. It was as if she'd never thought about this possibility. For her, Gourvec was still in his twenties, and certainly not a man who might get old or die.

"Why did you want to see me?" she asked.

"Well, I don't want to bother you, but I was hoping you might help me fill in a few blanks about his life."

"Why?"

"He created a rather strange library, and I'd like to ask you a few questions about his past."

"You told me you were his friend."

"…"

"Then again, he never did talk much. I remember lots of long silences. What did you want to know?"

"You only stayed with him for a few weeks before returning to Paris, is that right? But you'd just married him. Nobody in Crozon knows why you left."

"Ah yes… I imagine they must have wondered about it. And Jean-Pierre never told anyone… that doesn't surprise me. It's so long ago, all of that. So, I can tell you the truth: we weren't really a couple."

254

"Not really a couple? I don't understand. I thought you wrote each other love letters."

"That's what we told everyone. But Jean-Pierre never wrote me a single word."

"…"

Rouche had imagined those impassioned letters as the ultimate proof of the book's authorship. This news put him out, even if it didn't necessarily change anything. Everything still pointed to Gourvec being the author.

"Not a single letter?" he asked. "But did he write?"

"Write what?"

"Novels?"

"Not as far as I remember. He loved to read, though. All the time. He would spend whole evenings with his head buried in a book. He muttered as he read. Literature was his life. I liked listening to music, but he cherished silence. That was why we were so incompatible."

"So that's why you left?"

"No, not at all."

"Then why? And what do you mean when you say you weren't really a couple?"

"I don't know if I should tell you my life story. I don't even know who you are."

"I'm someone who thinks that your husband wrote a novel after you separated."

"A novel? I don't understand. You just asked me if Jean-Pierre wrote, when apparently you already knew the answer. This is all very confusing."

"That's why I need your help—to understand."

Rouche pronounced these last words with intense sincerity, as he did every time he found himself at the heart of his investigation. Marina had developed an ability to hear the most private, the most real desires, and she had to admit that her visitor carried a very powerful feeling of hope within him. So she decided to tell him what she knew. And what she knew was the entire story of her life.

10

Marina Brücke was born in 1929 in Düsseldorf, Germany. She was raised to love her country and its chancellor. She spent the war years in a happy, golden bubble, surrounded by nannies. Her parents were hardly ever around: they were busy attending parties, travelling and dreaming. Each time they returned, Marina was ecstatic; she played with her mother and listened to her father's advice on how to behave. Their presence was rare but precious, and every evening Marina fell asleep with the hope that her parents would give her a kiss to last her through the night. But their attitude changed drastically; they seemed suddenly anxious. When they saw their daughter now, they paid her no attention. They became irascible, violent, lost. In 1945, they decided to flee Germany, abandoning the sixteen-year-old Marina to her fate.

In the end, she was placed in a boarding school run by French nuns; the convent was strict, but no worse than what she had known before. She quickly learnt to speak French fluently, and put all her energy into expunging all trace of her German accent. From snatches of conversation, she put together the truth about her parents, the atrocities they had committed. Hunted down and arrested, they were now in prison in a suburb of Berlin. Marina realized that she was the fruit of a love between two monsters. Worse, they had tried to stuff her head full of lies, and she felt soiled by the existence of such thoughts in her mind. She was disgusted by having been their child. Convent life gave her a chance to drown her personality in a relationship with God. She woke at dawn and worshipped a higher power, reciting the prayers she had learnt by heart. But she knew the truth: life was nothing but darkness.

When she turned eighteen, she decided to stay at the convent. In truth, she didn't know where else to go. She didn't want to become a nun; she just wanted to stay there until she had found some meaning in life. The years passed. In 1952, her parents were released, as part of the country's reconstruction. They immediately came to see their daughter. They didn't recognize her: she was a woman now. She didn't recognize them: they were shadows. She didn't listen to their regrets; she ran away—from them, and from the convent.

Marina wanted to go to Paris, a city that the nuns had spoken about as a place of wonders, and which had always appealed to her. When she arrived, she went to the offices of a Franco-German association she'd heard about. It was a small organization that attempted to create a link between the two countries, and to offer aid. Patrick, one of the volunteers, took the young woman under his wing. He found her a job, in the cloakroom of a large restaurant. Everything went well until the boss discovered that she was German; he called her a "dirty Kraut" and fired her on the spot. Patrick tried to get the boss to apologize for his actions, which made him furious: "What about my parents? Did *they* apologize for what they did to my parents?" This kind of attitude was common at the time. It was only seven years since the war had ended. Living in Paris, while constantly being associated with Germany's past, was still very complicated. But Marina couldn't imagine going back to her homeland. So Patrick made a suggestion: "You should marry a Frenchman, and your problems will be over. You speak French without an accent. With the right papers, nobody would ever know you were foreign." Marina agreed that this was a good idea, but she didn't see whom she could marry; there was no man in her life; in fact, there had never been a man in her life.

Patrick couldn't volunteer because he was engaged to Mireille, a tall redhead who would die eight years later in a car accident. But he thought of Jean-Pierre. Jean-Pierre Gourvec. A Breton man he'd known when they were doing military service together. A slightly odd guy, very introverted, chronically single, an unusual man who spent his life in books—he seemed exactly the kind of person who might agree to such a proposition. He sent him a letter explaining the situation, and Gourvec took no more than ten seconds to agree. As his friend had anticipated, the temptation was just too big:

marrying an unknown German woman was such a novelistic thing to do.

The agreement was sealed. Marina would go to Crozon, they would marry, stay together for a short while, and then she would leave whenever she wanted to. They would tell anyone who asked that they had met through a lonely hearts ad; they'd fallen in love through writing to each other. To start with, Marina was worried. It seemed too good to be true; what did this man want in return? To sleep with her? To make her his maid? She was apprehensive as she travelled to the west of France. Gourvec welcomed her quite casually, and she realized immediately that her fears were unfounded. She found him charming and shy. As for him, he thought she was incredibly beautiful. He hadn't even wondered about her appearance; he'd agreed to marry a stranger without asking for a physical description. After all, it wasn't real; it was a marriage in name only. But he was overwhelmed by her beauty.

She moved into his small apartment. She thought it gloomy and too full of books. The shelves looked fragile. She didn't want to die, crushed by the collected works of Dostoyevsky, she told him. Those words made Gourvec laugh; a rare event for him. The young librarian told his two first cousins (the only family he had left) that he was going to get married. The mayor asked Jean-Pierre and Marina to say yes, and they did, playing it for laughs. But white is still a colour, and they both felt an unexpected tremor in their hearts.

I I

The newlyweds started living together. Marina soon showed signs of boredom. Gourvec, who often ate at the Picks' pizzeria, had noticed Madeleine's pregnancy; he suggested that his wife help them at the restaurant, and so it was that Marina worked as a waitress for a few weeks. Like Gourvec, Pick was not a very chatty man; thankfully, Marina could talk with his wife. She quickly admitted that she was German. Madeleine was surprised—she would never have guessed from Marina's accent—but what intrigued her most of all at the time was the bride's joyless face; she imagined she didn't like living in the wilds of Finistère. Her expression changed whenever she mentioned Paris, its museums, its cafés, its jazz clubs. It wasn't difficult to guess that she would soon be gone. Yet she always spoke fondly of Gourvec, and even admitted one day: "He's the kindest man I've ever met."

And it was true. Without being extravagant, Gourvec lavished his wife with small kindnesses. He slept on the sofa, so she could have his bedroom. He often made dinner, and tried to share his love of seafood with her. After a few days, she learnt to adore oysters, having previously thought that she couldn't stand them. People can always change; their tastes are not fixed. Gourvec liked to watch Marina sometimes when she slept; it was one of his secrets. There was something enchanting about how childlike and innocent she looked when she was dreaming. For her part, Marina would sometimes read a book that Gourvec recommended; she wanted to join him in his world, attempting to bring a little reality to their shared life. She didn't understand why he made no attempt to seduce her; one day, she almost asked him: "Don't you find me attractive?", but she didn't. Their life together became the theatre of two opposing forces: a gradually growing attraction hindered by an impeccably respected distance.

Even though she dreamt of returning to Paris, Marina did let herself imagine what it would be like to live in Brittany. She could stay close to this reassuring, even-tempered man. She could finally put an end to her fears, to her exhausting search for peace of mind. However, one day she announced that she would soon be leaving. He replied that it was what she'd planned to do. Marina was taken aback by this reaction, which struck her as cold and unfeeling. She would have liked him to beg her to stay a little longer. A few words can change a life. Gourvec had those words deep inside him, but he was incapable of uttering them.

Their final evening was silent; they drank white wine and ate seafood. Between two oysters, Gourvec asked her: "What will you do in Paris?" She said she didn't really know. She would leave the next day, but at that precise moment this was all she knew; her future was as hazy to her as a mirage in a desert. "What about you?" she asked. He told her about the library he wanted to create in Crozon. It would probably take months of work. The evening ended after this polite conversation. But before going to sleep, they hugged briefly. This was the first and last time that they ever touched each other.

The next day, Marina left early, leaving a note on the table: "In Paris, I'll eat oysters and think of you. Thank you for everything... Marina."

<h2 style="text-align:center">12</h2>

They had loved each other, without daring to admit it. Marina waited in vain for a sign from Gourvec. The years passed and she ended up feeling completely French. Sometimes, she would add proudly: "I'm from Brittany." She worked in fashion, was lucky enough to meet the young Yves Saint Laurent, and ruined her eyes spending hours embroidering sophisticated bustiers for designer dresses. She had a few adventures, but for ten years she didn't have a single serious relationship; several times, she thought about going to see Gourvec, or at least writing to him, but she imagined that he probably had a girlfriend. In any case, he had never come to sign the divorce papers. How could she have imagined that Gourvec had never settled down with anyone after her departure?

In the mid-1960s she met an Italian man in the street. Elegant and playful, he reminded her of Marcello Mastroianni. She'd just seen Fellini's film *La Dolce Vita*, so she took this as a sign. Life could be sweet. Alessandro worked for a bank; its headquarters were in Milan, but it had branches in Paris too. He had to travel back and forth quite frequently. Marian liked the idea of being in an on-off relationship. For her, it was a way of gradually getting used to love. Each time he came to visit, they would go out, have fun, laugh together. He was like a prince who'd just come from his kingdom. Until the day when she discovered she was pregnant. Alessandro now had to accept his responsibilities and stay with her in France, or she could follow him to Italy. He told her that he would ask the bank to transfer him permanently to Paris, and he seemed thrilled at the idea of having a child with her. "And I'm sure it will be a boy! My dream!" Then he'd added: "We'll call him Hugo, after my grandfather." At that moment, Marina thought of Gourvec: she would have to contact him to get her divorce. But Alessandro was against all conventions, and he considered marriage an outmoded institution. So she said nothing, and watched as her belly grew big and round, filled with promises.

Alessandro's hunch was correct: Marina brought a boy into the world. When she gave birth, Alessandro was in Milan, finalising the details of his transfer. Back then, it was customary for men not to attend the birth; he would arrive the next day, probably weighed down by gifts. But the next day, he arrived in another form altogether—a telegram. "I'm sorry. I already have a wife and two children in Milan. Never forget that I love you. A."

So Marina raised her son on her own—without any family, and without a husband. And with the constant feeling that people were judging her. A single mother was looked down upon at the time; whispers followed her wherever she went. But that didn't really matter. Hugo was her courage and her strength. Their relationship was so close that it protected them from the rest of the world. A few years later, she started wearing glasses to correct her vision, but her ophthalmologist was pessimistic; tests revealed that she was gradually losing her sight, and would almost certainly end up blind. Hugo, then sixteen, thought to himself: if my mother can't see any more, I have to exist in some other way inside her mind. That was what led him to start playing the piano; his presence would be musical.

He practised and practised, and won first place in the entrance exam for the conservatoire, at more or less the exact moment that Marina became completely blind. As she couldn't work anyway, she went to all her son's rehearsals and concerts. At the start of his career, he decided to use Brücke as his stage name. It was a way of accepting who he was; this was his story, it was their story—his and his mother's—and it belonged to them. Brücke meant "bridge" in German. Marina realized then that her existence was composed of scattered elements, without any real connection, like islands that must be bridged artificially.

13

Rouche was stunned by this account of her life. After a while, he said: "I think Jean-Pierre Gourvec loved you. In fact, I think he may have loved you all his life."

"Why do you say that?"

"I told you: he wrote a novel. And I now know that the novel was inspired by you, by your departure, by all the things he could never tell you."

"You really think so?"

"Yes."

"What is the novel called?"

"*The Last Hours of a Love Affair*."

"Ah."

"Yes."

"I would love to read it," she said.

For the next two mornings, Rouche returned to Marina's room to read Gourvec's novel to her. He read it slowly. Sometimes, the old woman asked him to repeat certain passages. She punctuated them with a few remarks: "Yes, I recognize that. That's so like him…" As for the sensual, imaginary parts, she believed he'd written what he wished he could have lived. After living in darkness for so many years, she could understand this concept better than anyone. She was constantly creating stories to help her live vicariously what she couldn't see. She'd developed a sort of parallel life, similar to the lives created by novelists.

"And Pushkin? Did he ever mention him to you?" asked Rouche.

"No. That name means nothing to me. But Jean-Pierre loved biographies. I remember him telling me about Dostoyevsky's life. He liked to discover other people's fates."

"That's maybe why he mixed reality with a writer's life."

"It's very beautiful, anyway. The way he writes about dying… I could never have imagined he would write so well."

265

"He never talked to you about his dream of being a writer?"

"No."

"..."

"When did this novel come out?"

"He tried to have it published, but he didn't succeed. I have a feeling that he was hoping to come back to you in the form of a book."

"Come back to me..." echoed Marina, with a wobble of emotion in her voice.

Moved by the old woman's reaction, Rouche decided not to mention the book's publication for the moment. She didn't seem to have heard of its success. Better to give her time to digest this news, and the book itself. As Rouche was preparing to leave, Marina asked him to come closer. She took his hand and thanked him.

Just once, she shed a few tears. Here was another bridge in her life. The past coming back into the present, after decades of silence. All her life, she'd felt sure that Jean-Pierre hadn't loved her; he'd been generous, adorable, tender, but he hadn't shown the slightest indication of what he felt. His novel revealed his feelings, which had been so powerful that he had never loved another woman. She realized now that she had felt the same thing. So their love had existed, and perhaps that was all that really mattered. Yes, it had existed. Just like the luminous stories that she created in the heart of her darkness. Life has an inner dimension, with stories that have no basis in reality, but which are truly lived all the same.

14

When he decided to investigate this story, Rouche had guessed that it might have murky depths, but never could he have imagined that it would dredge up so many powerful emotions. Yet there was still something else important that he had to accomplish.

In his tiny attic, he slept for most of the afternoon. He dreamt that Marina was eating giant oysters that transformed into Brigitte yelling at him because of the car. He awoke with a start and noticed that night was falling. He took out his laptop and started trying to order his notes; he didn't yet know to which newspaper he would offer his article—maybe to the highest bidder?—but he felt certain that the literary world would be excited by his revelations. All the same, he didn't want to question the integrity of Éditions Grasset; all the evidence suggested that the publishers had sincerely believed Pick to be the author.

After working on the piece for almost two hours, he received a text. "I'm in the café downstairs. I'm waiting for you… Joséphine." His first reaction was to wonder how she knew his address, before remembering that he'd told her where he lived during their nocturnal conversation. His second reaction was to think that he might not have been home that evening. It was a little strange to wait downstairs from someone's apartment without warning them in advance. But then he thought: in her eyes, I'm the kind of man who has nothing to do except stay at home in the evenings. And, when he thought about this, he realized that she was right.

He replied: "I'll be there very soon." But it took him longer than he'd expected. He didn't know what to wear. Not that he wanted Joséphine to find him attractive, but… well, he didn't want her to find him unattractive. When he first encountered her, reading her interviews, he'd thought she was a bit of an idiot. After meeting her at the cemetery, he'd quickly changed his mind. He thought about all of this, standing in front of his wardrobe, as he sank ever deeper into indecision. At that precise moment, he received a second message: "Come as you are. It'll be fine."

15

They were drinking red wine together. Rouche had wanted to order a beer, but in the end he'd followed Joséphine's lead. While he was wondering what clothes to wear, he'd daydreamed that some irresistible urge had driven her to seek him out. Perhaps she had come to confess her feelings for him. This was not the most plausible hypothesis,[23] but he had reached a point where nothing would surprise him. After some small talk, during which they stopped calling each other *vous* and started using the more intimate *tu* form, Joséphine explained the reason for her presence.

"I don't want you to publish your article."

23 It had been a long time since a woman had driven three hundred kilometres to see him without warning. In fact, it had never happened before.

"Why? I thought you and your mother wanted the truth to come out. I thought you were sick of this whole story."

"Yes, that's true. We wanted to know. And, thanks to you, we now know that my father didn't write that novel. You can't imagine how shaken we were by this whole thing. We felt as if we'd been living with a stranger all those years."

"I understand. But telling the truth would bring things back the way they were."

"No, it wouldn't. It would just rile everybody up again. I can already imagine the journalists asking me: 'How does it make you feel to learn that your father didn't actually write that novel?' It would never end. And I think it would be humiliating for my mother, who went on television to talk about the novel. She would look ridiculous."

"I don't know what to tell you. I thought it was important to tell the truth."

"But what will it change? Nobody cares whether it was Pick or Gourvec. People liked the idea that it was my father. Just leave it like that. Besides, it would cause problems."

"Why?"

"Gourvec has no heir. Grasset wouldn't pay us the royalties."

"Ah, so that's what this is about."

"It's *one* of the things this is about. What's wrong with that? But I can promise you that, even if there were less money at stake, I would still ask you the same thing. This whole story has caused me too much pain. I don't want to talk about it any more. I want to move on. So, yes, that's what I'm asking you. Please."

"…"

"…"

"You see, I met Gourvec's wife," said Rouche. "It was very emotional. I read her the novel, and she realized that Gourvec really loved her."

"Well, there you go, that was your mission. That's wonderful. You should stop there."

"…"

"If you like, I could give you a nice present," said Joséphine, grinning in an attempt to defuse the tension.

"You want to buy my silence?"

"You know it's better for everybody this way. So, go on… what's your price?"

"Let me think about it."

"Just name it."

"You."

"Me? Come on, don't dream. I'm much too expensive. You'd have to sell a lot of books before you could hope to have me."

"All right, then… a car. Would you buy me a Volvo?"

The conversation went on until the café closed. It didn't take Joséphine long to convince Rouche. He'd always thought that his investigation would lead to an important change in his life. That was what was happening, though not in the way he'd expected. They seemed to understand each other so perfectly. Joséphine announced that she hadn't booked a hotel room. Like him, she was apparently the kind of person who didn't plan their accommodation in advance. They went up to his apartment, and he was not afraid of her judging it as he might have been with another woman. They lay down side by side, but this time in the same bed.

16

The next morning, Joséphine suggested that he come with her to Rennes. After all, there was nothing left for Rouche in Paris. He could start a new life, perhaps working in a library or writing articles for the local newspaper. He liked the idea of a fresh start. They drove slowly along the motorway, listening to music. After a while, they stopped for a coffee. As they drank, they realized that they were falling in love. They were the same age, and they were no longer interested in appearances. The first hours of a love affair, thought Rouche. It was wonderful to drink this undrinkable coffee in a gloomy service station, and to know that there was nowhere else in the world he would rather be.

EPILOGUE

I

FRÉDÉRIC LIKED to put his ear to Delphine's belly, hoping to hear a small heart beating. It was still too early for that. They had already drawn up endless lists of names. It was obvious they were going to find it hard to agree, so the writer suggested a deal to his wife: "If it's a boy, you can choose. If it's a girl, the choice is mine."

2

A few days after this pact, Frédéric announced that he had finally finished his novel. Until now, he had not wanted to show any of it to his editor, because he wanted her to discover it in its entirety. With a certain apprehension, she picked up *The Man Who Told the Truth* and locked herself in the bedroom. She came out barely an hour later, her face curdled in fury. "You can't do this!"

"Of course I can. This was the plan."

"But we talked about it. You agreed!"

"I changed my mind. I need everybody to know. I can't keep silent about it any longer."

"This is going too far. You know that we would lose everything."

"You might. I won't."

"What does that mean? We're a couple. We have to make decisions together."

"It's easy for you. You have everything."

"I'm warning you, Frédéric. If you decide to publish this book, I'll have an abortion."

He was speechless. How could she say such a thing? To use their child's life as a bargaining chip in a disagreement… It was vile. She realized she had gone too far, and tried to patch things up. Moving closer to Frédéric, she apologized. In a softer voice, she asked him to think this through. He promised he would. In the end, the awful nature of the blackmail she had attempted made him understand just how fearful she was of losing everything. And she was right: the world would judge her harshly for her scheming. And particularly for having convinced an old lady that her husband had written a novel. Her anger was surely justified. But he had to think about himself. That was only reasonable. He'd been champing at the bit for months, thinking only of that moment: when everybody learnt the truth. At last, the world would know that he was the author of this bestselling novel. She could always respond that what people had loved, most of all, was the novel behind the novel: the pizzeria owner who'd written in absolute secrecy; perhaps this was true, but without his novel, there would be no novel behind the novel. And now she was asking him to keep quiet. He had to remain hidden behind his puppet.

3

It had all happened quite simply. Frédéric had accompanied Delphine to Crozon for the first time, several months before. He'd met her adorable parents, discovered the charms of Brittany, and every morning he had stayed in the bedroom to write. The title of his book was *The Bed*, but nobody really knew what it was about. Frédéric always preferred to write in secret, believing that to divulge the contents of a novel in progress was to endanger it. He was finishing writing the story of a separating couple, with Pushkin's death throes as a backdrop. He was very enthusiastic about this idea, and hoped that this second novel would be more successful than the first. But that seemed unlikely: apart from a few authors, not necessarily the best ones, hardly anybody sold books these days.

After a conversation with Delphine's parents, they went to visit the famous library of rejected books. That was where he had the idea of making people believe that his new novel had been discovered here; it would be a brilliant marketing plan. And, once sales had taken off, he could announce that he was the author. He shared his idea with Delphine, who agreed that it was excellent. But according to her, the manuscript needed an author; not an invented name or a pseudonym, but a real person. That would intrigue everybody. On this point, events would prove her right.

They went to the cemetery in Crozon and chose a dead person to be the book's author. After some hesitation, they opted for Pick, because both of them were fond of writers with a K in their name. He had died two years before, and was in no position to contradict their version of events. But they would have to inform his family and get them to sign a contract. Having done that, nobody could possibly suspect fraud. Frédéric seemed surprised by this, but Delphine explained to him: "You won't receive the money for this book, but once everybody knows you're the author, you'll be famous, and that will have repercussions for your next novel. It's best to go all the way with this. Nobody except the two of us should know the truth."

Frédéric took another few days to revise his novel. He thought it possible that Delphine's mother might have seen his manuscript, with the title *The Bed*, so as a precaution he opted to change the title. He also changed the typeface, to make it look as if it had been written on a typewriter. The young couple printed it out, and tried to weather the paper, to make it look older. Once they'd done this, they went back to the library with this literary treasure that they pretended to discover there.

When they presented the story to Madeleine and she reacted sceptically, they thought it would be a good idea to manufacture a sort of proof. So it was that, during their second visit, Frédéric hid the book by Pushkin among Henri Pick's belongings after saying that he needed to use the bathroom. They had sown their seeds now. But they could never have anticipated what would grow from them. The book's success surpassed all their hopes, but it also trapped them, in a way. Delphine realized this after the programme presented by

François Busnel. Viewers had been so moved by Madeleine that it was now impossible to tell the truth without appearing to be heartless manipulators. This was terrible for Frédéric, who had to hide the fact that he was the author of the best-selling book in France, and to accept his status as an author whose ex-girlfriend hadn't even heard of his first novel. While Delphine was crowned with all the glory, he brooded on the injustice of it all and decided to write a novel revealing the truth. In this book, he not only recounted the details of the affair, but gave a philosophical analysis of our society's obsession with form over substance.

4

Frédéric accepted Delphine's apologies, and admitted that he would be putting them in danger if he revealed the fraud they had perpetrated. A few days later, at the start of their summer holidays, they decided to go to Crozon.

In the mornings, Frédéric stayed in bed and tried to write a new novel, but it was hard. Sometimes he would go out alone and walk along the seafront. During those times, he would think about the last days of Richard Brautigan in Bolinas, on the misty California coastline. The American writer, his career in decline, had sunk into a mire of alcohol and paranoia. For several days, he was out of contact with everybody, even his daughter. He died alone. His body was already decomposing when it was found.

During that stay, Frédéric decided to visit the library in Crozon. The place where this whole story had begun. He saw Magali and noticed that there was something different about her, although he couldn't put his finger on what had altered in her appearance. Perhaps she had lost weight? She welcomed him warmly.

"Ah, it's the writer! Hello there!"

"Hello."

"How are you? Here on holiday?"

"Yes. And we'll probably stay several months. Delphine is pregnant."

"Congratulations! A boy or a girl?"

"We don't want to know."

"Ah, so it'll be a surprise."

"Yes."

"And have you written a new book?"

"I'm getting there, slowly."

"Well, let me know when it's coming out. We'll order copies here, of course. You promise?"

"I promise."

"Actually, while I've got you… if you're staying in Crozon for a while, how would you feel about running a writing workshop?"

"Um… I don't know…"

"Just once a week, max. With the retirement home next door. They'd be so thrilled to have a writer like you."

"I'll think about it."

"Oh, that'd be great. To help them write their memoirs, you know."

"Okay, we'll see. Anyway, I'm going to look around. I'll probably borrow a book."

"Wonderful," said Magali, smiling as if he'd just paid her a compliment.

Frédéric headed over to the bookshelves, thinking over the offer she'd just made. When his first manuscript had been accepted for publication, he'd imagined himself surrounded by young female fans, receiving literary prizes, perhaps even the Goncourt or the Renaudot. He'd also thought that his books would be translated all over the world, and that he'd travel through Asia and America. Readers would eagerly await his next novel, and he'd be friends with other great writers. He'd thought all of this, but he hadn't imagined that he would end up helping elderly people to write, in a small town in the wilds of Brittany. Surprisingly, this idea made him smile. He couldn't wait to tell Delphine about it; he loved being close to her. And he was going to be a father. He realized, even more forcefully now, that the prospect filled him with joy.

5

A few minutes later, he took the manuscript of *The Man Who Told the Truth* from his bag and left it in the library of rejected books.

THE NEXT BOOK IN THE
WALTER PRESENTS LIBRARY

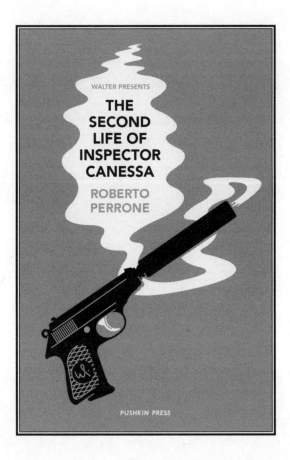

PUSHKIN PRESS

Pushkin Press was founded in 1997, and publishes novels, essays, memoirs, children's books—everything from timeless classics to the urgent and contemporary.

Our books represent exciting, high-quality writing from around the world: we publish some of the twentieth century's most widely acclaimed, brilliant authors such as Stefan Zweig, Marcel Aymé, Teffi, Antal Szerb, Gaito Gazdanov and Yasushi Inoue, as well as compelling and award-winning contemporary writers, including Andrés Neuman, Edith Pearlman, Eka Kurniawan, Ayelet Gundar-Goshen and Chigozie Obioma.

Pushkin Press publishes the world's best stories, to be read and read again. To discover more, visit www.pushkinpress.com.

━━━

THE SPECTRE OF ALEXANDER WOLF

GAITO GAZDANOV

'A mesmerising work of literature' Antony Beevor

SUMMER BEFORE THE DARK

VOLKER WEIDERMANN

'For such a slim book to convey with such poignancy the extinction of a generation of "Great Europeans" is a triumph' *Sunday Telegraph*

MESSAGES FROM A LOST WORLD

STEFAN ZWEIG

'At a time of monetary crisis and political disorder... Zweig's celebration of the brotherhood of peoples reminds us that there is another way' *The Nation*

THE EVENINGS

GERARD REVE

'Not only a masterpiece but a cornerstone manqué of modern European literature' Tim Parks, *Guardian*